PUFFIN BOOKS
Editor: Kaye Webb
Fairy Tales by Alison Ut

Everyone who has read any of Alison Uttley's books, maybe
about those favourite characters Little Grey Rabbit, Little
Red Fox or Sam Pig, will know the dear enchantment called
forth by her from every flower and stick and stone of the
countryside she loved so much. But they may not know that
she was also the author of several books of fairy stories,
and that it was in these stories that her faculty for rich and
romantic enchantment reached its fullest power.

Kathleen Lines has chosen her favourite stories from all
these books for this selection, and they all share this famous
author's delicious appreciation of country scenes and people,
and an even more heightened feeling than usual of the magic
there is in all country things.

As we read of the woodcutter's daughter Cherry-blossom
and 'the golden bear in the great cave of the fire', the snow
maiden who loved the little boy who made her, the goose
girl who flew in a hammock made by her geese from their
own wings, or even the day Grandfather-Clock and Cuckoo-
Clock left time behind and went jaunting off on holiday,
we can only marvel and rejoice at the highly personal
imagination which helped her turn the sights and sounds she
so dearly loved into the reality of fairy things.

As well as the books about Sam Pig and Little Red Fox
published in Young Puffins, we have two books for older
readers, *A Traveller in Time* and *The Country Child*, which is
the story of Alison Uttley's own childhood.

Fairy Tales
by Alison Uttley

Chosen by Kathleen Lines

Illustrated by Ann Strugnell

Puffin Books
in association with Faber and Faber

Puffin Books, Penguin Books Ltd,
Harmondsworth, Middlesex, England
Penguin Books, 625 Madison Avenue,
New York, New York 10022, U.S.A.
Penguin Books Australia Ltd, Ringwood,
Victoria, Australia
Penguin Books Canada Ltd, 2801 John Street,
Markham, Ontario, Canada L3R 1B4
Penguin Books (N.Z.) Ltd, 182–190 Wairau Road,
Auckland 10, New Zealand

This collection first published by Faber and Faber Limited 1975
Published in Puffin Books 1979

This collection copyright © Faber and Faber Limited, 1975
Illustrations copyright © Faber and Faber Limited, 1975
All rights reserved

Made and printed in Great Britain by
Richard Clay (The Chaucer Press) Ltd
Bungay, Suffolk
Set in Linotype Baskerville

Contents

Contents

Foreword

These stories are taken from Alison Uttley's many collections of fairy tales, the first of which, *Moonshine and Magic*, appeared in 1932 and the most recent, *Lavender Shoes*, in 1970. The stories are truly 'fairy tales' in that they reveal, to the willing eye and ear, the usually unsuspected magic in the countryside and in the lives of humble village people. The traditional 'princess' is a beautiful country maiden, the 'prince' a fine, upstanding shepherd or farm labourer, whose rival in love is either a member of the fairy folk or a manifestation of some natural force.

Although many of the stories have their roots in folk tales, and a few seem 'translations' of well-known stories, all of them show the unmistakable characteristics of Alison Uttley's treatment and style. They also give proof of an amazingly long span of imaginative writing.

Mrs Uttley said of her fairy tales: 'So each and every tale holds everyday magic, and each is connected with awareness of everyday life, when reality is made visible, and one sees what goes on with new eyes.'

KATHLEEN LINES

The Woodcutter's Daughter

In an old thatched cottage deep in the forest lived the woodcutter, Thomas Furze, and Margaret his wife. They were a homely couple, simple and hardworking. All they wanted was a child, and at last their wish was granted. Late in life, a little girl was born to them.

She was as pretty and dainty a little creature as they were plain and weather-beaten. They gazed upon her with rapture, as if a small angel had come to earth. Her cheeks were pink as the cherries in the wild wood, her skin was white as cherry blossom, and her lips as sweet as honeystalks. So the child was christened by the romantic name of Cherry-blossom, with Cherry for short.

The father was the romantic one of that family, for the mother was practical and matter-of-fact. Between them they managed not to spoil the little girl, and they brought her up very sensibly, considering all things.

Little Cherry helped her mother in the cottage even when she was very tiny. She went to the village school through the clearing in the wood, and her father took her part of the way, past the goblin trees and haunted dells. At night she sat by the fire, listening to the tales he told her while he carved strange beasts from the curiously shaped bits of wood he brought back from the forest. He always had an eye for odd things, and he noticed that some boughs were shaped like animals, and that faces sometimes seemed to peer from a crooked tree trunk.

The stories he told were very exciting and real to the little girl. He spoke of dragons that once lived on earth, of fairies like brilliant winged people flying in the air, and mermaids dwelling in the coral sea. Cherry never wanted a book to read while she could hear such legends and folk tales. As her father talked in his low voice, and her mother's knitting-needles clicked, half-impatiently, the girl saw princes and peris, fairies and elves, inhabiting a world beyond the radiant moon, yet close to her own forest home.

As she grew taller and older, and perhaps a little wiser, she hid the fairy tales in a corner of her heart, and she left the village school. She had to earn her living, but the good people did not want her to leave home. So she put a little card, printed in neat characters with her own pen and ink, in the front parlour window.

'Good plain sewing and ladies' stuffs made up', it said, for all the world to read. The only ones who saw it were the tawny squirrels who ran along the low garden fence, and the robin hopping by the door.

However, there was soon plenty of sewing to be done, for Cherry's mother spoke to her own friends in the town and they told their mistresses and patrons. Once in three months Cherry went to this town, walk-

ing many a mile, and sometimes getting a lift in the
carrier's cart for part of the way. She stayed the night
at her grandmother's, a very ancient woman nearing
ninety. She collected sewing to be done from the
ladies, who admired the neat tiny stitches of the forest
girl. At any rate, they said, her mother had taught her
to sew, down there in the back woods.

They gave her chemises and petticoats to make
from fine linen, to be tucked and gathered, feather-
stitched and button-holed, ruffled and pleated, and
the threads drawn in lovely patterns. There were
handkerchiefs to be hemstitched and lace caps to be
made. Cherry packed her parcels in a bundle, bound
them with a cord, and carried them on her back to the
cottage.

Then she worked hard with her needle, stitching
the dainty work for the fine ladies, sewing her hopes
and desires and dreams into the linen, embroidering
her fancies on the edges with many a smile at her in-
most thoughts.

One night when her parents had gone to bed, the
girl sat late finishing a piece of work. Her needle
flashed in and out of the white linen, and she leaned
close to see her stitches. The lamp flickered out, and
as there was no paraffin in the barrel in the house corner, she lighted a candle and finished by its slender
beam. Then she sat by the fire, staring into the
depths, half-dreaming, watching the golden castles in
the flames, the towers that glowed and smouldered
and fell with a silent clatter of gilded walls. She gazed
at the flames, jagged like the antlers of the stags in the

forest. They were soft as fur, they blew together in pointed tongues. They changed before her eyes, and lo! there was a golden bear in the great cave of the fire.

The girl stared bewitched at the lovely wonder of it, fearing the beautiful beast would disappear like all the marvels of enchantment in the world of fire. But he stayed there, walking slowly through the gateway of the caves and under the arches of gold. Outside, the wind howled like a wolf, it snarled and snapped, and the forest whined back. The door shook, and the shuttered windows rattled and bumped as an icy blast swept through the crannies and caught up the flames.

Cherry was afraid the fire would break up, and the

pattern of mystery dissolve, but the bear came down the glowing embers, stepping silently along a track in the flame. It grew larger, its fur quivered, it raised its head and walked out of the fire, and stood on the wide hearthstone, its shaggy feet on the sanded stone.

It shook itself and sparks flew about the room. Its golden eyes gazed at her, questioning her. The girl sprang to her feet in terror and started for the door, but the bear spoke softly to her. Its voice was deep as the wind when it rumbles in the hollows of caves. Its eyes were filled with supplication. Its head was lowered before her in submission.

'Woodcutter's daughter. Give me a drink of cold water, I pray you of your mercy,' it said.

Cherry ran to the bucket of spring water standing on the sink, and she carried it to the hearth. The bear drank and drank, and its colour ebbed and flowed, from gold to black, as the coldness of the water touched it.

'Woodcutter's daughter. Give me food, I pray you of your charity,' said the bear.

She went to the cupboard and brought out a honey-comb and a newly-baked loaf, which she put on a platter for the bear. It ate with enjoyment, finishing every morsel, while she watched, fascinated.

'Woodcutter's daughter, what is your name?' asked the bear.

'Cherry, if you please,' she answered. 'Cherry-blossom I was christened, but they all call me Cherry for short.'

The bear looked around, at the little kitchen, at the

young girl, at the white sewing heaped on the oak table near the guttering candle.

'Cherry-red, cherry-white, cherry-blossom on the tree. Will you make a coat for me?' asked the bear, chanting and swaying as it spoke.

'A coat?' she cried, surprised and puzzled.

'Make me a green coat from the nettles in the cherry grove in yon woods,' said the bear.

'I know where you mean, but – but – I don't think I can sew nettles,' she hesitated.

'Stitch it finely and closely and bring it here for me,' said the bear.

'Well, I'll try,' said Cherry, 'but I've never stitched nettles before. Only linen and lace. Not nettles.'

The bear was already moving back into the fire, stepping across the hearthstone, growing smaller, walking into the heart of the flames. Deep in the fire Cherry saw the bear with a thin chain round its neck led by a sprite to the cave. It faded away, the fire burned up with a fierce rush, and she waited. She took the poker and stirred the cave. With a crash it fell, and the cherrywood log lay over the place, hiding everything.

'Am I dreaming, or did I really see a bear?' she asked herself. The empty water-bucket stood on the hearth, and the platter beside it. There was a loaf missing from the cupboard, and the honeycomb gone. She packed up her sewing, took her candle, and went slowly up to bed.

'Father, I dreamed that a great golden bear came out of the fire,' she said the next morning.

'Ah! That's a lucky omen. Such dreams come when you burn cherrywood. I've been cutting down some of those great wild cherry trees in the clearing among the nettles. They are very ancient trees and some of them are hollow. That's where I found that wild bees' honeycomb.'

'Where is that honeycomb, Cherry? I can't find it. I thought we had four loaves of bread, too, and there are only three,' cried Mrs Furze, peering in the bread-mug.

'Mother, I gave them to the bear, in my dream,' stammered Cherry.

'You gave them to a bear? Whatever do you mean?' exclaimed her mother.

'Don't ye bother her, Mother,' said the placid woodcutter. 'This is a strange happening. I've heard of it before, long ago, when I was a little 'un. It has happened afore, and it brings good luck, they say.'

No more was said, for Mrs Furze was a sensible woman. Cherry went out to the grove where her father was thinning old cherry trees. She gathered a great basketful of nettles, which was nothing unusual, for those simple people had nettle broth and boiled nettles as vegetables many days in the spring when their garden had no green stuff.

The woodcutter left his work and joined his pretty daughter.

'See here, Cherry lass,' said he, taking her arm and leading her to a place where the nettles were thickest. 'Look here. This carved stone has meant something once upon a time.'

He showed her a broken pillar of marble, carved with grapes and leaves and strange outlandish beasts.

'There's an old story told that many many years ago a castle stood here, in this clearing. It is country talk that wherever the nettles grow, there was once a dwelling for man. Nowhere in this forest are there nettles save here, among these broken stones and cherry trees.'

'Yes, Father. I know,' said Cherry. 'I used to play under these wild cherry trees when I was coming home from school. I found many a piece of marble carving. I love this spot, Father.'

'The cherry trees must have been in the castle grounds,' continued her father, poking about in the rubble. 'Nobody living knows what happened, or re-members anything about it. Your grandmother knew the tale, but her parents could not remember the castle.'

He returned to his work and Cherry took the nettles home. She began to stitch them together with some hesitation at first and then with an eagerness to succeed in the task. Nettles are thick and fibrous, covered with tiny hairs that sting, but a good grasp overcomes the sharp prickles of poison. The girl sewed every night when her parents were in bed. She dare not let them see what she was making. A coat of nettles for a bear! They would think she was crazed. Although her father would perhaps understand, her mother would scold, so she kept the work secret.

Each night she went to the oak press and took out the nettle coat. She stitched more leaves to it, using tiny stitches and sewing with extreme care and delicacy.

Many a time she went back to the clearing for more nettles, and as she gathered them she exposed the old foundations of the castle. She could trace the rooms, the great hall, the hearth which was under a yew tree, and the courtyard, where four cherry trees grew. Beyond was the orchard, where the older trees spread their aged branches, and gardens, all wild with primrose and dog roses.

Although she made many inquiries when she went to the town with her bundle of finished garments, nobody could tell her anything of the dwelling that had once stood there.

Sometimes when she sewed the green coat, the golden bear came out of the fire and lay on the hearthstone by her side. Round his neck was a chain. He never spoke, except once when he asked again for food and water. He did not answer her questions. He lay with his head on his paws, watching her, and she felt strangely happy when he was with her. Then back he lumbered into the fire, and the thin black sprite caught him and led him into the golden caves.

The coat sleeves were finished, the lapels stitched, and the two large hunting pockets were fixed to the sides. It was a grand coat, fit for a real hunter to wear, with plenty of room for game in those pockets. Cherry spread it out on the floor and looked to see if anything were missing. There were no buttons, of course, and she wondered whether to put some bone buttons from her mother's work-box down the front. She made three large button-holes ready.

Then she took her needle and some threads of her own silky gold hair and embroidered flowers of the dead-nettle down the front. It was an extra, something special, for the bear's pleasure.

That night she saw three golden buttons glowing in the heart of the fire. She raked them out, and left them to cool on the hearth. Then she stitched them on to the embroidered front of the coat and waited, for she was certain the bear would appear.

Out of the fire he walked, getting larger and larger, till he stood, a great golden bear, by her side.

'It is well done,' said he. 'Put the coat away till the time comes. Keep it safe until I am ready.'

'When will that be?' she asked, disappointed that nothing happened.

'A few more months,' he replied. 'Now you must make yourself a dress, beautiful as snow. Make a dress fit for a queen.'

'How can I?' she laughed. 'I have no stuff for a dress, and I couldn't wear one of nettles.'

'Make it of cherry blossom, like your name,' said the bear, and he went into the fire without another word.

The next day Cherry went to the woods for the flowers of the wild cherry. The trees were full of bloom, but the petals soon fall, and there was little time left before they would all be gone. She carried a basketful of flowers home and set to work at her dress.

As she could only work at night, she sewed all through the long hours. It was easier than the nettle coat, for the bunches of flowers clung together with a few stitches, and soon she had a complete dress, sweet-scented and exquisite. The flowers did not fade, they stayed fresh as when they were gathered. Cherry spread out the dress for the bear to see.

Out from the fire he came and praised her work. 'A little longer,' said he. 'I must wait till winter comes, and the fire roars up the chimney. Keep the cherry-blossom dress and the nettle coat near you till I come again. Be ready for me. You can save me, and only you.'

Many days passed and although Cherry looked into the fire each night there was no golden bear in the caves. The flames danced in the fireplace, the smoke, blue as a gentian, billowed among the trees. Cherry sat sewing her ladies' garments. Sometimes she went out to the woods, to visit the deserted castle, with its wild cherry trees, red-gold in the autumn.

'When winter comes I shall see my bear,' she thought. 'I shall be glad to see him. I miss his company. When he came from the fire and lay by my side, how happy I was! Is it possible to love an animal with all one's heart?'

One winter morning she got ready early to visit the town. Her work was completed, and it was time to take it back before Christmas.

'I wish I could come with you, my dear,' said her mother. 'It is too far for me to walk, but you can carry a basket of eggs to your grandmother, and give her our love. Take care of yourself, child.'

Cherry kissed her mother, and walked away in deep content, with her basket and bundle, for there had been a sprinkling of snow in the night, and the woods were very beautiful. She passed through the grove of old cherry trees, and they seemed to be in blossom. Each tree had round bunches of snow hanging on the knotted boughs, in clusters like real flowers. The shape of the castle walls was clearly outlined by the snow, and she stayed a few minutes to rest there, before she went on her journey. Under the yew tree the ground was clean and dry, with a carpet of yew needles. She thought she saw a shadow pass, and there were footprints in the snow of some large animal. There were chippings of wood left by her father, and she drew them together in a spirit of make believe, and piled them on the hearth. She placed four carved bits of stone round the kindling wood.

'Father can boil his can of tea here, when he comes,' she said to herself. 'He will know I got it ready for him.'

Then away she walked, with quick light step, laughing to herself as she thought of his surprise. She had brought the nettle coat and the cherry dress in a parcel to show to her grandmother, and this also made her light-hearted. Surely the gold bear would not mind if such an old woman saw what she had made. If she had seen him, she would have asked permission, but it was several months since he had appeared in the fire. Perhaps when she got back home, he would be there. Her heart was warm with the thought of him.

She wore a blue handkerchief tied round her hair, and a thick brown cloak over her old blue frock. Her clothes were shabby, but in the woods they seemed to be exactly right. The snow shadows were blue, and the misty distances were azure, and the tree trunks were brown. The girl went along like a living shadow, moving swiftly in and out of the beeches and oaks and hollies. The carrier's cart never appeared, and she had to walk the whole way to the town. That made her late, and she went straight to her grandmother's house, and rested there for the night.

She showed the old lady the delicate sewing she carried in her pack, but she kept back the nettle coat and the cherry-blossom dress in sudden shyness. She told the news of the forest, how her father had built a new shed by the house, and a squirrel had come to live in it, and the deer had broken into the garden one night, and the pig had been killed to make bacon for the winter months. She gave her grandmother a little carved egg-cup her father had sent, and the eggs from her mother, and some brawn she had made and chitterlings. Still she hesitated to mention the nettle coat and the cherry-blossom dress.

'Did you see anything in the forest when you came through?' asked the grandmother in quavering tones.

'Oh yes. I saw many things, Grandmother. Green woodpeckers, and the deer, and red squirrels, and a white owl, half asleep in a tree and —'

'Nay, not those things, child. Did you see any

queer things? Any strange unco' things?' persisted the grandmother.

'Why yes, Grandmother. I saw the trees all silvered with snow, the dark faces in the trunk of that tree I know very well. Like a gnome it is, all wrinkled and large-mouthed. I saw a shadow move once, in the wild cherry grove. I stayed there a minute among the trees in the clearing where there are carved stones, and, do you know, the trees seemed to be covered with cherry blossom, even in the middle of winter!'

'There's something else,' said the old woman slowly. 'A bear has been seen. A golden bear, they say. The hunters are after him. Yellow-gold fur, and gold eyes he has. They are after him.'

'I'm not afraid of a bear,' said Cherry. 'I saw one in the fire. A golden bear, right in the flames, and he came out to me.'

'Ah! I saw a bear in the fire long ago. It was there in the middle of the fire, and there it stayed. It's a lucky sign, they say. A bear in the fire is a piece of good luck waiting for you, but it's different from one outside in the wood. It might catch you.'

The old woman wandered on, and Cherry was half asleep. She decided not to show her nettle coat but only the blossom dress, to her grandmother.

'I made this, Grandmother,' said she, turning the skirt and bodice of snowy petals on the rug and shaking out the folds. 'Do you like it?'

The grandmother touched the lovely blossom with a shaking finger.

'Is it your wedding dress, my child?' she asked.

'I don't know, Grandmother. I made it out of the cherry blossom growing on the wild trees in our wood,' said Cherry.

'Who are you going to marry, Cherry?'

'Nobody has asked me, Grandmother.'

'This must be your own wedding dress, my Cherry,' said the grandmother. 'I was asked to make a flower-petal dress when I was a girl, but I never made it.'

'Who asked you, Grandmother?' asked Cherry, softly.

'One in a dream, I think. I heard a voice as I sat by the fire, and I never forgot. Life would have been different if I had hearkened and made it, I reckon.'

She shook her head, and went off to sleep.

The next day Cherry called at the houses of the rich ladies, the goldsmith's wife, the clergyman's wife, the banker's lady, and the brewer's lady. She received her payment, and the new sewing to be done. They thanked her in their high hard voices, they shook their silken skirts, and sat in their fine rooms as she stood before them in her shabby clothes and took their orders.

'Mind you sew neatly. Take care you don't soil this silk. This is soft as a flower. You have doubtless never had such fine materials, girl,' they said.

'Once I sewed flower petals,' said Cherry, curtsying.

'Nonsense. Nobody can sew flower petals,' they scolded. There was quite a heap of linen and silk with gold threads woven in it, and soft wools, fine as cobwebs. Cherry's fame had spread and many ladies wanted the woodcutter's daughter to make their clothes, to stitch her pretty pattern on their shifts and nightgowns and petticoats.

It was late before Cherry had collected all the work to be done, but she knew her mother would be anxious if she stayed another night. She wrapped her money in her handkerchief, and stored it in her bosom. She carried the bundle on her back, tied up in layers of cloth to keep the stuffs clean. In her hand she had a lantern and the small packet with the nettle coat and the cherry-blossom dress.

'You won't get home till after dark, Cherry love,' sighed the grandmother, and she gave her a loaf of bread and cheese for the journey, and a pannikin of tea.

'I shall be safe, Grandmother,' said Cherry, kissing her on her withered soft cheeks.

'Mind that golden bear. Don't let him catch you. God be with you.'

'And God be with you, Grandmother,' said Cherry.

She waved the lantern and started off down the road. When she got to the forest she lighted the lantern and walked through the beech trees on the narrow track she knew so well. But the lantern threw strange deceiving shadows as she got deeper into the woods, the trees seemed to be moving this way and that, advancing and retreating to confuse her, and the pathway was hidden in snow. She went on for some miles, then the snow began to fall again, dancing flakes rushed to meet her, blinding her eyes, catching in her hair, lying on the pack till it was heavy as lead.

She struggled on, tired and sleepy, finding her way

by the stars, until the snow hid the sky. She realized she was lost, and the only thing to do was to find a shelter and wait till morning. She went on, bewildered by the snow, seeking a tree where she could rest. She was unafraid, for she had often been in the forest at night, and she knew there was nothing to harm her. Then she saw the dark branches of a yew, and her feet stumbled against the stones on the ground. She knew where she was, and this could be no other place than the ruins of the old castle, two or three miles from her home.

Her lantern light fell on the heap of wood she had collected the day before, when she started off for the town. In a minute she had lighted it, and was warming her frozen hands at the blaze. She sat down in the warmth and shelter of the ancient yew tree, and spread out her wet cloak and scarf to dry. The yew needles were soft as a bed under her feet, and she leaned against the red scaly trunk of the tree, and unfastened the bundle with the nettle cloak and the cherry-blossom dress. They were crumpled and flattened, but she shook them so that the petals were fresh, and the nettles were stiff and shapely. Then she hung the two garments in the yew tree, and busied herself, warming her tea in the little pannikin, throwing more wood on the blaze.

The crackle of the fire was so cheerful, she laughed aloud with pleasure.

'Here I am, drinking tea in the ruined castle, and soon I shall be at home. I know my way blindfold from here. What a tale to tell!'

She was startled by the distant sound of shots, and in a minute a great golden bear came towards her, his side bleeding, his eyes half glazed with pain.

'My bear. My golden bear,' she cried, running to him. She tore up her scarf and bound it round him. She opened the linen pack and took the choicest pieces to wrap on his wounds.

'Drink this,' she said, and she poured out the rest of her tea, and offered him food. He shook his head, and lay down by her side.

Then she heard the noise of approaching hooves, and shouts of men. They had seen the light, and were coming nearer, nearer.

'Into the fire! Quick, or they will catch you,' she cried.

'I escaped from the fire, Cherry-blossom, and now you send me back,' he said.

'It's your only chance,' said Cherry, urgently.

The bear stood by the crackling flames for a moment, and his blood made a pool on the ground. Then he entered the fire, and even as the flames touched him, he became smaller and disappeared in the leaping tongues.

The huntsmen galloped up, surrounding the tree.

'Which way did that bear go? He must have passed quite close. See – his blood is here. He might have killed you, for he was wounded and dangerous,' they shouted.

'He went out of sight. He disappeared,' said Cherry, standing with her back to the fire.

'And what are you doing here, a young girl alone

in the forest at night?' asked one of the men, as the others galloped off.

'I am Cherry, the woodcutter's daughter. This is where my father has been cutting wood. I got lost coming from the town, and I am going home,' explained Cherry.

'Then get on my horse and ride with me, Cherry, for you are a pretty girl, and I shall enjoy taking you home,' said the young man.

'No, sir.' Cherry thought of her bear, caught in his woodland fire.

'What? You don't want to go home? Then I shall stay here and take care of you. It isn't safe with a bear in the woods,' he said impudently, and he flung himself from his horse, tied it to a branch of the tree, and sat down by the fire. He threw fresh boughs on it, and Cherry stood looking anxiously at him. Far away they could hear the horses galloping.

'Now tell me what you are doing here in the forest,' he continued. 'That wounded bear came very close to you. Here is its blood.'

Even as he spoke, pointing to the ground, Cherry could see the golden bear moving in the flames. She went towards the man, lest he should notice, but the horse was aware of the presence of the wild beast. It reared and plunged in terror, neighing shrilly.

'What's the matter with you?' called the man, but he went to calm it. 'The bear must be somewhere near, he's so frightened.'

'Oh, golden bear! Come out and rescue me,' whispered Cherry, leaning to the fire.

Out from the flames stepped the bear, growing tall and splendid as he left the fire, but already the horse had broken away and the man ran after it.

'Throw the nettle coat into the fire,' commanded the bear. 'Throw it into the flames, now.'

She tossed the green coat upon the burning wood, expecting to see it shrivel up. The leaves were burnt away, but the strong fibre of the nettles remained. It became a coat of gold, a web of gleaming threads like a coat of mail. The bear picked it from the embers and put it on his shoulders. Immediately he changed to a man, tall and fair, strong and valiant.

'Now throw your cherry-petal dress on the fire,' commanded the bear-man, pointing to the white dress hanging in the yew tree.

Cherry obeyed, and the dress became white as silver, with every petal clear and bright.

'Wear it, Cherry. It is for your wedding. Now look around.'

Then Cherry saw that she was standing in the hall of the castle, and the yew tree was the wide chimney stack, growing up, with dark boughs curving to the roof. The fire glowed on the hearth, shining up to the great timbers of the roof, to the lovely branches of the tree. The floor was covered with the carpet of yew needles, and seats of carved stone and rugs of fur were in their places. Through the high windows of the spreading yew tree Cherry could see the stars, and at the far end there was a great door of carved wood.

'All this was destroyed hundreds of years ago,' said the bear-man. 'My enemy broke the castle walls and enchanted me, so that nobody knew what had happened. In a night all disappeared, and the memory of the place went. Into the flames I was cast and I was held there until a girl should release me. I became a bear of fire, doomed to lie in the gold cave, from which I could come forth at times to seek a rescuer. I tried to escape, but nobody helped me, until I found you. You made me the burning coat of nettles which had sprung up from the bones of my home. You brought my home to life again by lighting this fire on the hearthstone, from which it had been banished for centuries. You sat in the hall and played in the castle when you were a little child, among the broken stones. I loved you then, as I watched you with the cherry blossom falling upon your hair. I saw you unafraid, playing your childish games in my house.'

'Yes,' said Cherry, staring round with wonder and delight. 'I used to play here. I always thought there was somebody watching me, sharing my games. I never felt alone.'

'Woodcutter's daughter, will you marry me?' asked the bear-man.

'Yes, golden bear,' said Cherry. 'I will marry you.'

'We will go back to your father and mother and bring them here to the castle. For long years I have been like one dead, held within the fire by the spirit of evil. Now I am alive and I love you, Cherry-blossom.'

'And I love you, golden bear,' answered Cherry, holding up her face to his.

He put his arms around her, and down upon their

heads fell a shower of snow which was cherry petals.
The cherry trees in the grove were in flower again
that winter's day. The turtle dove cooed in the
boughs of the yew tree, and a charm of goldfinches
flew across the open chamber. Together the bear-man
and Cherry-blossom walked out into the moonlit
wood, to the thatched cottage of the old people. They
looked back, and in the place of the cherry wood
stood a great house, white as snow, shining like fire,
with a yew tree rising from its walls.

The Bird of Time

A white-bearded ancient man walked over the hills and wide valleys of the world. On his back he carried a sack which moved uneasily as if something were trying to escape from it, but he settled it between his shoulders and plodded along unwearied, with even strides, and unvarying pace, taking no account of the lands through which he went.

He was Father Time, travelling for ever, and the sack he bore was filled with To-morrows, all struggling and shuffling to get out.

Each night, at twelve o'clock, he opened the bag and out flew a To-morrow, just one, with its wings of blue, and its shining feathers rosy with hope. All the rest were kept back by Time's strong hands and pushed deep in the sack.

Down flew the To-morrow, beating its lovely feathers, but as it touched the earth off fell its blue wings and it changed to an ordinary white bird which could not fly. It had become a To-day. Every one knows that To-day isn't as wonderful as To-morrow, for To-days can be held in one's hands, accepted, despised, scorned, but To-morrow is full of mystery and beauty. It holds fortune and happiness. It is desired by all the world. Even those with little hope sigh, 'To-morrow may bring a change. To-morrow life will be different.'

Everybody tried to catch the To-morrow before it fell to the ground, so that they could peer under those blue wings and rosy feathers, to see what the future brought for them. Some To-morrows bore Happiness and Love under their wings, others carried Grief and Poverty, but all was hidden until To-day came.

The people thought if they knew beforehand what the To-morrow carried they could prepare for it. So they put bird-lime on the trees where the To-morrows might alight as they flew from Father Time's bag, and they hunted the birds with great nets, seeking to capture one before he changed his plumage. Yet although they tried every device, the birds escaped them and flew to the ground as To-days.

At last, after many experiments and failures, a Philosopher caught a To-morrow. He made a web of dreams and wove it tightly into a net. This he spread in the air, and behold! a To-morrow fluttering down was caught! He took it home, struggling, and fluttering its blue wings and rosy feathers, but it could not get out of the closely woven meshes. He suspended the net from the ceiling of his room, and watched the bird. Its wings were dazzling with promises, each one of a deep-blue colour, and as the bird shook its feathers the promises sprayed the air. Each wing had twelve long pinions, and they were To-morrow's hours. Every feather in the pinion was To-morrow's

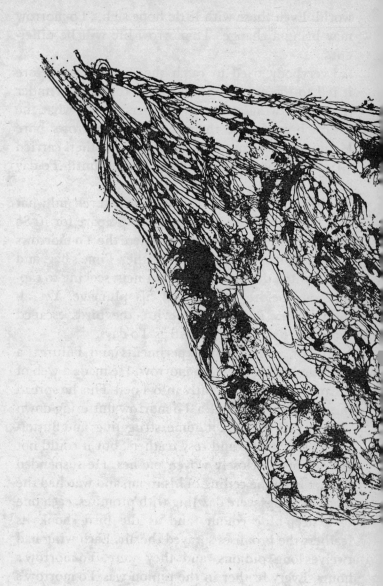

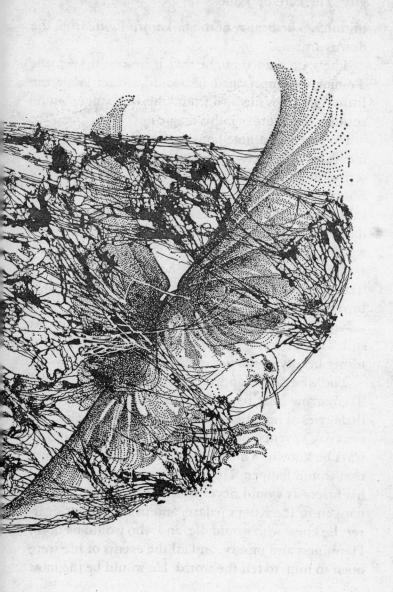

minutes. The beauty of the unknown shone from the downy breast.

The wise man thought that if he could keep the To-morrow imprisoned he would always know the future. Perhaps the bird would die, or change, but he could catch another in his magic net.

He took out a note-book and a tape-measure, and measured the pretty creature. He wrote down a description of the changing iridescent colours, as the minutes and hours went by, and he wrote too the promises he could see for every minute of time the next day. All day he wrote, setting down everything that would happen on the morrow. At midnight he waited, for then Father Time would set free another To-morrow, a new bird. He watched to see if his own bird would become a To-day, white as snow.

No, its wings sparkled with fresh promises, it was still To-morrow, lovely To-morrow, waiting in glittering beauty in the net.

The wise man clapped his hands with joy, and the To-morrow beat its wings and tried to escape with little cries of impatience, but the net held firmly. The next day's events could be read, To-morrow would always be known. The wise man now knew everything that would happen. He could foretell the future and his forecasts would never fail. He knew what would happen in the King's palace, and in the beggar's garret; he knew who would die, and who would be born. Happiness and misery, and all the events of life were open to him, to tell the world. He would be the most powerful of all men — yet he kept his secret a little longer.

Each day he feverishly wrote the future happenings, and always the words were true, so that he knew all things. But as he looked at the changing feathers of the beautiful bird, he felt sad. He wanted to warn people of their fate. If he told the sorrows of To-morrow, he would spoil To-day, he would break even the white bird, To-day; whilst if he spoke of the happiness To-morrow would bring, he would lessen the joy of unexpectedness.

He decided to invite people to see his wonderful bird, to judge for themselves whether they would know all things. So he opened his doors and welcomed any who wished to view a beautiful To-morrow.

People came crowding in, rich and poor, all eager to see To-morrow. They pressed round the exquisite shy bird, which flew gently to and fro in the net of dreams, never resting its feet, with no perch or branch, its feathers gleaming like a changing rainbow. As they read the future in the moving wings of To-morrow, their cries of excitement grew louder, they pushed and struggled to get nearer. Some wept, others groaned, whilst many laughed wildly and tried to seize the bird with upthrust greedy hands, eager for more news. The bird flew out of their reach, and the wise man came back to keep it from death at their hands.

Out of doors he sent the crowd, and they streamed down the roads to their homes, shouting, wild-eyed, frightened, for only a few were strong enough to bear either the good or the evil in store for them.

The wise man locked his doors and returned sadly to the room where the blue-winged To-morrow fluttered slowly in the net of dreams. There, standing underneath it, with a hand thrust through the meshes of the net, was a little boy who had been left behind.

As the child stroked the soft plumage, and spoke with endearing words to the lovely creature, the bird stretched its wings to their utmost, and broke the net. It flew down to the ground, and the wise man never attempted to catch it, but watched intently to see the blue wings fall, and the feathers change. To his surprise it remained the same radiant colour. It was a bird of To-day, with wings of blue and feathers rosy with hope.

'There are no To-morrows for a child,' said the philosopher, thoughtfully, as he watched the bird preen itself whilst the boy kneeled down and stroked its wings. 'To-day is the most perfect time and To-morrow is unknown and undesired.'

'Keep it,' said he to the eager boy. 'It is yours for ever.'

He unlocked the doors and threw them wide open. The child walked out of the house with the bird in his arms, a lovely To-day, a beautiful bird which never changed till the boy grew to be a man. Then it fluttered its blue wings and darted up into the sky to find its master, Father Time. But the young man sat down at his desk and wrote a poem about it.

The Four Brothers

Once upon a time, and that was very long ago, there
lived a young girl named Sally. She had brown eyes
and short dark hair, brushed like a boy's, and she was
a chatterbox and a teaser. She lived at an inn, the
'Hope and Anchor', an old timbered inn by the side
of the great highway which goes to London one way,
and to Scotland the other. It wasn't an ordinary inn,
for Sally's father was an old sailor who had sailed
round Cape Horn, and been to the China Seas. He
wore gold earrings in his brown ears, and his beard
was golden too, pointed in a triangle, like Drake's.

In the garden he had a tall mast with a flag atop,
and he hauled it up and let it down with ropes, and
used strange sailor talk, such as country folk don't
understand. There was a wooden figurehead of a
heathen god, Neptune, leaning against the rockery
under the fir trees, and this made all the little children come and stare and run away as fast as they
could, for they thought the wooden man would catch
them.

The inside of the inn was as clean as a pin, everything scrubbed white as a bone, and polished till you
could see your face in it. That was Sally's task and the

young servant girl's, for these two did nearly all the work between them. On the dresser was a model of a cutter, and on the mantelpiece were curious foreign shells, which roared like the waves of the sea when you held them to your ears. Hanging over the window was a sailing-ship in a quart bottle, and this brought many a penny to the old sailor's pocket, as he showed his customers and told them yarns of the sea.

Sally was very proud of being a sailor's daughter, and the village children thought of her as a princess. They made her leader in their games, and she was chosen to be the May Queen when the first of May came round, all because her father was a sailorman in that village where hardly anyone had even seen the sea.

She had four brothers who were going to be sailors when they were old enough. Full of pranks they were, stealing apples from the orchards, climbing the haystacks, hanging the village washing on the treetops. They played tricks on the customers, too, did Matthew, Mark, Luke and John, whose saintly names were misplaced for such young scamps.

One of them had a frog-mug. Do you know what that is? A brown earthenware mug with a little green frog at the bottom. Matthew filled it with ale and gave it to an unsuspecting customer, who drank till he saw the frog's eyes staring at him, and its shiny back appear. Then there was a shout and great laughter at the joke.

More than anything they delighted in riddles, and these pleased the countrymen, whose minds were stored with old quips and jests, for this happened in days when there were few books, and riddle-telling was the winter's pastime.

'I went to the wood and got it. I sat down to look for it. I brought it home because I couldn't find it. What's that?' asked Matthew.

'A thorn,' said the sailor, when no one could guess.

'In what place did the cock crow, when all the world could hear it?' asked Mark.

'On Noah's Ark,' said somebody.

'What does a seventy-four-gun ship weigh, with all her men on board, just before she sails?' asked Luke.

This was given up, and John told them: 'Her anchor.' Then the mugs of ale went round, tankards were filled afresh, songs were sung, and the 'Hope and Anchor' got a reputation for wit and understanding.

When the four brothers were old enough, they all went to sea, and the village returned to its quiet ways, missing their pranks and noise. Sally was left alone with her father, for her mother had died when she was born. She cooked pease-pudding, and baked the bread and made cowslip wine and cherry-brandy. She spun the snowy sheep's-wool on her spinning-wheel, and dyed the wool blue, and knitted her brothers each a pair of stockings ready for their return from their voyage to foreign parts.

'What will they bring me when they come back?' she asked her father.

'Oh, I don't know. Something queer, I expect,' he answered, staring into the red fire. 'Perhaps a poll parrot, same as I brought your mother, or a lump of coral, or an idol, or some silk.' Sally went about her work, singing and sighing a little, and thinking very often of her four brave brothers over the sea.

After two years a letter came for Sally. Letters were rare events in those days, and Sally and her father broke the red seals, and spread out the paper on the little oak table in the bar-parlour, with a group of friends to listen to the news.

'My dear Sister Sally,' went the letter. 'We have had a good voyage, and seen some whales. I am bringing you a present. It is a goose without any bone. Your affec. brother, Matthew.'

'A goose without a bone!' exclaimed Sally. 'What a present! What kind of bird will that be? Can it walk?'

'It must be some strange foreigner, perhaps a Chinese goose,' said the linen-draper, and he turned over the letter and stared at the broken seals with their emblem of the rising sun.

'Where shall I keep the goose without any bone?' asked Sally. 'I hope it will be able to swim in the duck pond.'

She went about her work thinking of the queer bird which was coming over the sea, and all the village chattered and wondered. A parrot or a cockatoo would have been a nice gift for Sally, but a goose without any bone! Really, it was too silly! Only the old

sailor was silent, with a secret smile as he listened to the talk.

A few weeks later there came another letter for Sally, and this had a blue seal, stamped with a ship in full sail. The girl opened it quickly and held it to the parlour window where geraniums and hanging white bells grew.

'Dear Sister Sally,' said the letter. 'We have had a good voyage, and seen some dolphins. I am bringing you a present when I come home. It is a cherry without any stone. Your affec. brother, Mark.'

'A cherry without any stone!' cried Sally. 'That's an odd present! I love cherries, but all cherries have stones. It isn't much to bring me all that way, is it, Father?' The sailor agreed that it wasn't much of a present, but 'Wait and see,' he advised.

'It's some outlandish foreign fruit your brother has found, although I never heard tell of a stoneless cherry, and I'm a man of considerable knowledge,' said the squire's gardener. Sally polished and scrubbed, and thought of the soft rosy cherries her brother Mark was bringing to her in a great sailing ship.

Now there came a third letter, with a green seal, and a ship's anchor on it. 'This'll be from Luke,' said Sally as she ran and called her father, and took it to the light.

'My dear Sister Sally,' she read. 'We have sailed round the world and seen some yellow men. I am bringing you a fine present. It is a blanket without any thread! Your affec. brother, Luke.'

Sally read it three times, and then she looked at her smiling father. 'Oh dear!' she sighed. 'How Luke teases! That won't be warm at all,' and all the customers in the bar-parlour repeated: 'No warmth in that, Miss Sally! A blanket without any thread. Did you ever hear the like? Fancy that!' and they banged their mugs on the polished tables and asked for more of the nut-brown ale.

'It must be some kind of blanket they use in hot countries,' explained the schoolmaster. 'A tropical blanket, to keep off the flies,' and all week Sally dreamed of a cobweb blanket hanging on a palm tree.

Finally a fourth letter came, a large square letter, sealed with a black seal, and a flying seagull upon it.

'This is brother John's writing,' said Sally, contentedly, as she opened the letter. 'He is more sensible than the others. I wonder what he will bring for me.'

She read the letter aloud to her father and the company, all seated in the sunshine by the open door. 'My dear Sister Sally,' it said. 'We are coming home soon after you get this. We have had a grand voyage and seen a sea-serpent. I am bringing you a beautiful present. It is a book no man can read. Your affec. brother, John.'

Sally stamped her foot. 'What is the use of that?' she cried. 'A book no man can read. Why can't my brothers be serious?'

'Perhaps it's written in some foreign tongue, Greek, or double-Dutch,' said the cobbler, and they all shook their heads over the strange odd languages

in the world, which men spoke when they might talk
honest English.

So Sally repeated:

> *A goose without any bone,*
> *A cherry without any stone,*
> *A blanket without any thread,*
> *A book no man can read.*

They listened open-mouthed, and recalled the
pranks and tricks the brothers had played when they
were at home.

'Depend upon it, there is some joke in this, some
mystification,' said the old cobbler, who knew more
than the schoolmaster and the parson. The sailor
nodded his head and smiled. 'Maybe,' he agreed.

One fine day, up the hill which led to the inn came
four sailor lads, with their trousers a-swinging, and
their jaunty caps aslant on their heads, and their
bundles slung on their backs. Sally ran out to meet
them and flung her arms round each, kissing and clip-
ping them all soundly. After her came the old sailor
himself, full of laughter and joy to see his four sons
again.

'You teasers!' cried Sally, when they had put their
bundles on the floor, and stretched their legs by the
house fire. 'Where are those strange presents? We've
all puzzled our heads off with wondering what they
were. Where are the cherry and bird, the blanket and
book?'

'Coming up in the tranter's cart,' replied John,

winking at the others. 'A blanket without any thread is heavy, you know.' They all grinned, and Sally hugged him, happy to have him at home again.

Soon the bar-parlour of the 'Hope and Anchor' was filled with men who had come in to drink the healths of the returned brothers, and Sally and the maid were kept busy running to and fro with the pewter tankards and earthenware mugs. There was a rumble of wheels at the door, and the tranter's cart came up.

'Now sit you still, Sally my dear, and we'll bring our presents in to you,' said John, pushing her into the armchair, and the four boys went outside.

'Now we shall see,' said the cobbler. 'Now our eyes will be opened.' He drank his ale and stood up ready to clap.

Matthew came in, carrying something hidden in his hands.

'The first is a goose without any bone,' said Sally, as he stepped across the room to her.

'When the goose is in the eggshell there is no bone,' said Matthew, and he held out a fine goose-egg to his amazed sister.

Next came Mark, with his mocking smile and twinkling blue eyes. 'What was my present, Sally?' he asked, as he stood in the doorway, his hands hidden.

'The second is a cherry without any stone,' replied Sally.

'When the cherry's in blossom there is no stone,' said Mark, and he held out a small cherry tree covered with snowy-petalled flowers, growing in a beautiful

Eastern pot. Sally gave a cry of joy, and put it on the window-sill.

Then Luke put his head in at the door and muffled sounds came from outside, as if something struggled to get free.

'What was my present, Sally?' he asked, and his merry black eyes gleamed with amusement.

'The third is a blanket without any thread,' said Sally.

Luke walked into the room leading a great white ram with amber eyes and a thick curly fleece on its back.

'When the fleece is on the sheep's back there is no thread,' said the boy, and the ram jingled the bell at its neck and shook its horned head at the company of men, who laughed and shouted and clapped their hands.

Finally John came in, young John with his brown hair, and bright kind eyes. 'What was mine, Sally love?' he asked.

'The fourth is a book no man can read,' said Sally, who looked like the Queen of Sheba with her gifts around her.

Then John bore in a little printing-press, with all the letters backward. 'When the book is in the press no man can read,' said he, and everyone crowded round to look at the treasure, and to guess what was the tale in the press which no man could read.

Now the foreign goose-egg was set under the broody hen and in due time a wonderful gosling hatched out. It grew into the finest goose imaginable, with scarlet legs and snow-white wings, and a crest of red feathers on its head. It laid an egg every day, which the old sailor had fried for his breakfast. Yes — it was indeed a fine goose!

The cherry tree was planted in the garden, and every spring it had masses of delicate blossoms, and every summer it was covered with rich fruit, different from country cherries, as full of sweetness as a hive is full of honey. Although there was never a stone in the flower, each cherry had a round hard heart.

The ram provided many a blanket from its heavy wool and it lived in the little square field at the back of the inn for many years. The inn has long since been pulled down, but the name of the field remains to remind us of this famous ram, for it is called 'Blanket Croft' to this day.

As for the press, the story when printed was a strange tale of the Arabian Nights. Sally used it later to print her own little tales. One of the first she wrote was this, and the brothers sang it with her on Saturday nights to the visitors who came to see the wonders:

> *I had four brothers over the sea,*
> *And they each brought a present unto me.*
> *The first brought a goose without any bone,*
> *The second a cherry without any stone,*
> *The third a blanket without any thread,*
> *The fourth a book no man can read.*
> *When the cherry's in blossom there is no stone.*

When the goose is in egg there is no bone,
When the wool's on the ram's back there is no
thread,
When the book's in the press, no man can read.

But the old sailor smiled to himself more than ever.
'I just know'd 'em all along,' said he. 'I guessed 'em,
every one of 'em,' and he filled the frog-mug with his
home-brewed ale and drank it up.

The Companion

In the cottage down by the side of the canal lived a girl. Her father was the lock-keeper, and he looked after the narrow bridge which spanned the canal. When a canal boat was seen in the distance moving smoothly over the green glassy water, he swung the little wooden bridge back against the bank and waited. Then the boat sailed through, and the barge-woman waved her hand, and the great horse which pulled the barge shook its head and nodded to him. Then the little girl, whose name was Betty, ran from the cottage down by the water's edge and stared with longing at the boat with its coloured funnel, and its pot of geraniums.

'I should like to live in a canal boat,' she thought. One day she pulled open the drawer of the chest in the kitchen just opposite the open door by the canal side, and she took out a clean cotton frock, and starched blue sun-bonnet. She dressed herself neatly and she leaned over the water to look at herself.

There were no looking-glasses in that house, for the last was broken some years before, and they had had seven years of bad luck, so her mother said.

'We don't want any more bad years,' said Mrs But-
ters. 'So we'll go without a glass. There's the water
at the door, as still and quiet as a mirror and that's
good enough for us.' So the little girl leant down and
gazed at her pink cheeks and her dark eyes reflected
in the water. Down in the water she saw a heap of
gold coins and guarding the treasure was a little green
frog. She ran for her fishing net to drag up the hoard,
but the water only broke into waves and rippled to
and fro so that the gold seemed to be broken into a
thousand pieces. The frog put forth a little thin hand
and leaned over his treasure, staring up at the face
above him and the wavering net.

'What are you doing, child, in your best cotton
frock?' cried the girl's mother.

'Oh Mother, I'm fishing for gold. There's a heap of
gold down here,' cried Betty.

'My child,' said the mother leaning over with a
smile. 'Nay, that's not gold. It's only the reflection of
the sunshine.'

'Oh Mother, I'm sure it's gold. See the little frog
guarding it,' said Betty eagerly, and she swished her
net up and down in the water till there was nothing to
be seen but the crooked waves with their glint of sunlight dancing on them.

'There's only the water weeds swinging down
there,' said her mother, and she turned back to the
house.

The little girl sadly drifted after her, but she went
again and again to the water's edge to peer down for
the gold. Winter was coming, the canal was dull and

the wind blew with bitter cuts like a carving knife, and gradually the fairy gold was forgotten in the ice and snow of winter.

Then with spring came a change. The rushes threw up new spikes, the water weeds returned with fresh new green. A few green leaves came up on stiff stalks, and they floated on the water. Each day they grew larger and stronger, and then buds appeared, round and hard as marbles. A speck of gold lay in the greenish petals, which unfurled in the sun and showed the buttercup flowers of the great noble kingcup.

'There's your fairy gold,' said the mother. 'I've never seen kingcups blowing on our canal side, but it's quiet and shallow here, and the water forget-me-nots live, so why shouldn't kingcups?'

Mother and daughter touched the big glossy leaves and the gold cups of the flowers, and the little green frog swam up and lay on a leaf as if it were on a raft.

One day as Betty knelt by the water, admiring the flowers, there was a movement by her side, and when she turned there knelt a girl exactly like herself.

The two stared at each other, Betty in amazement, the girl with a friendly look.

'Who are you? You're like me, just the same as me,' stammered Betty.

'I'm your reflection, your double,' laughed the girl in a faint voice like the breath of the wind. 'I can't speak except in a whisper, but I am here to be your friend if you want me. I heard your wish for the fairy gold and I've brought you a gold penny.'

She leaned across and picked one of the kingcup

flowers. It changed into a gold coin in her hand. It had the emblem of water engraved on it, a ripple of waves on one side and the sign of the Zodiac for water, Aquarius with his water cans, on the other.

'Mother, Mother,' called Betty, but she was silent as her mother appeared at the door.

'Yes, Betty. What's the matter?' asked the mother calmly, with never a glance at the girl at Betty's side.

'Look who's here, Mother,' said Betty.

'Who's here? Who is here? You shouldn't be so fanciful, Betty. There's nobody except – except a kind of light, from the water. It shines that way when the sun catches it and sends it on the trees.'

Betty was silent. She stared at the girl, who put a finger to her lips. So she must keep the girl a secret, she was not visible to her mother.

'Come for a walk with me,' she said to the girl and the girl nodded and ran by her side along the canal path. 'I'll show you the kingfisher and the waterhens,' said Betty.

'I know them all,' laughed the girl softly. 'They are my friends already. They know me too, they can see me when human beings are blind. Your mother is blind, too, Betty, but she will see me some day, I hope.'

They ran along together, racing past the barge which moved by the canal, touching the horse's flanks with their fingers, smiling at the cat sitting on board. Both cat and horse saw the girl and each made a sound of recognition, a cry and a grunt.

'What is your name?' asked Betty. 'Is it like mine?'

'No, I am called Caro, because the things love me,' said the girl.

'What things?' asked Betty.

'Everything, water and light and sunshine and air,' replied Caro gaily and she flung her arms up and seemed to catch the air in her hands. Then she stooped to the water and picked up a handful of drops which she let fall as dark stars on the pathway. They lay like flowers and they took root and grew in the grassy verge.

Then she saw the kingfisher. Instead of flying like a blue arrow across the water and disappearing in the distance he came near and perched on a low branch of a naked willow. The two girls stooped to him. Betty tried to touch him but he flew a few inches away so that Caro's hand could stroke his bright feathers. Then off he went, dipping and flying, to the river in the meadows.

Caro held up a tiny blue feather in her hands. She gave it to her companion.

'A present for you,' said she.

As Betty held it she could hear the voice of the bird flying over the river. It spoke to the wind and the sky, and it sang a few notes to the swallows dipping over the water. Kingfisher, blue halcyon bird, beloved bringer of luck to the fisherman and the little girl wandering by the canal.

'I heard what he said,' murmured Betty.

'Yes, the feather gives you the power to hear bird talk,' replied the reflection girl, diving into the water and returning dry as her companion. She brought up

a twig with a caddis clinging to it. They both leaned
over and admired the creature, and then the reflection girl dropped it back in the water, for overhead
flew a green dragonfly, singing and darting close to
the hair of the reflection girl.

'It thinks I am made of water,' she laughed and she
caught it in her fingers.

'Here's a green dragon for you, Betty,' said she.

The wings fluttered and the dragonfly sat on the band of light. Then it rose and flew away, with a bead of light on its head like a crown jewel of diamonds.

A horse stood by the fence as they wandered along the path. Betty called to it, but its eyes were staring at the girl by her side. Suddenly it kicked up its heels and laid its ears flat and dashed away.

'It's frightened of me,' said Caro. 'It can see me and it isn't quite sure. All animals can see the half-visible, only man is blind to them. And you, Betty, can see me.'

'You will go home with me, won't you?' asked Betty.

'No, your mother would not believe in me, I should be invisible to her, and she would think you were ill or crazed. No, better to keep me a secret. I am your sister, your reflection and you can always call me from the water if you stoop down and beckon to me.'

So when they got back to the cottage the girl gently slid back into the water, but before she did so she peeped into the kitchen. Betty's mother was busy setting the table for dinner.

'Come along, Betty,' she cried. 'You can set the table. There's a light by your side, a queer patch of sunshine came in with you. Shut the door. No, leave it open, it's pretty.'

She stared at the patch of sunlight, and the girl, Caro, slid back through the door, and away to the water.

So every day the girl came from the canal to play with the little girl in the cottage, and together they roamed the country, speaking to bird and animal and tree, finding flowers and insects and stroking the butterflies which always flew down to the reflection and settled on her watery shining hands.

The two remained friends and companions for years until Betty was grown up. On her wedding day Caro would not come when Betty peeped at her reflection in her wedding dress. But there was a white-veiled face in the water and many voices rang in the air singing a wedding chant.

'Praise light, O world of birds. Praise the blue light and the blue shadow, the sun and the moon, O birds. Praise them,' sang a voice in the water.

'Praise water, O creatures of the deep water. Praise the drops and the imprisoned sunrays and the moonshine and water weeds. Praise water,' sang the little water beetles and the dancing gnats and the minnows and caddis.

'Praise air, and sunlight and the shining threads which the spiders weave, and the tiny drops of dew,' sang the butterflies, as they dropped on her hands and wavered their wings like coloured fans.

'Praise God,' said the reflection as she dropped back in the water. 'Praise him for making a double for you to see, a soul and a spirit for you to play with, a hidden being down in the water's depths, to rise out and speak to you.'

The Spice Woman

> *Nutmegs and Cinnamon,*
> *Ginger and Caraway,*
> *Spice from the Indies,*
> *Buy, come buy.*

The old spice woman sang this song as she walked down the street with her scented basket on her arm, and her staff in her hand. Wafts of sweet-smelling breezes from far-away islands came from her basket and floated around her. Invisible branches laden with flowers and tropical fruits swayed over her head. Blue seas lapped her feet, and the murmur of the waves accompanied her lilting chant. These things were only dreams, but a warm tide of happiness came from her heart as she sang:

> *Nutmegs and Cinnamon,*
> *Ginger and Caraway,*
> *Spice from the Indies,*
> *Buy, come buy.*

In the King's kitchen there was a great cakemaking. Mrs Dumbledore, the cook, was making teacakes, and when she looked in the wooden nutmeg box, it was empty. Through the open window she heard the voice of the old spice woman, and the rich smell of her wares came into the room.

'Run quickly and get a crown's worth of nutmegs,' said she to the little kitchen-maid, Betsy. 'The spice woman only comes once a year, and I must have my box filled.' She took from her fat purse a silver crown, and off trotted little Betsy in her wooden shoes clop-clopping across the palace yard, past the red and gold sentry who guarded the gate, to the old spice woman, who walked down the street, her basket on her arm and happiness in her heart.

'And what can I do for you, my dear?' she asked, holding out the basket with the starched white napkin lying on the top.

'A crown's worth of nutmegs for Mrs Dumbledore, if you please, Mistress Spice,' said Betsy, demurely, and she dropped a curtsey and held out her money.

The old woman put the nutmegs in a sugarcone bag, and gave them to the dimpled girl. Then, with her blue eyes twinkling with merriment, she held out a little green nutmeg in her wrinkled hand.

'Here's a nutmeg for your own self, so keep it by you, my dear,' said she kindly, and Betsy curtsied, and blushed, and ran back to the palace to Mrs Dumble-dore, who waited impatiently with her sleeves rolled up and the nutmeg-grater in her hand. Soon the tea-cakes were in the oven, and when the Queen tasted them she vowed they were the most romantic cakes she had ever had.

But Betsy hid her own little nutmeg away in the

tin trunk under the attic roof, and there it lay between her pocket handkerchiefs, waiting for her to take it home.

A year later the old spice woman came down the street with her basket on her arm. She had walked hundreds of miles up and down many a country since she had last been outside the palace, but never had anybody given her such a pretty curtsey, or spoken so nicely, as Betsy. She was thinking of her now as she sang:

> *Nutmegs and Cinnamon,*
> *Ginger and Caraway,*
> *Spice for the Palace,*
> *Buy, come buy.*

At that very moment Mrs Dumbledore, with cheeks flaming from the kitchen fire, peered in the pewter cinnamon box.

'Goodness me! We've no cinnamon,' she cried, throwing up her hands. 'I have these cinnamon buns to make for Her Majesty, by special order, and there's nothing to flavour them. Take this crown, Betsy, and run out to the old spice woman before she gets away.'

So Betsy upped with her little blue gown and ran as fast as she could, right out of the palace kitchen,

across the yard, clop-clopping in her wooden shoes,
past the tall grand sentry, to the bent old woman,
who walked the streets with the basket on her arm
and happiness in her heart.

'And what do you wish for to-day, my dear?' she
asked, and she held out the basket with its snowy
linen on the top.

'A crown's worth of cinnamon sticks for Mrs Dumbledore, if you please, Mistress Spice,' said Betsy, and
she curtsied and smiled at the old woman as if she
were Her Majesty herself.

'Here's the cinnamon for Mrs Dumbledore,' said
the old woman, as she wrapped up the golden-brown
sticks in a paper, 'and I am giving you a stick of cinnamon for your own self. Take care of it, my dear.'

She held out a slender stick like a green branch,
sweet-scented and rich, and Betsy thanked her, smiling and bobbing in her tucked-up blue skirt. Then
back she hurried to the scolding cook, who soon made
a batch of delicious cinnamon buns for the Queen.

Betsy carried her cinnamon stick upstairs, to the
tiny room in the tower attic, and she put it at the bottom of her tin trunk with the nutmeg. She peeped
through the narrow window at the red-roofed town
below and the country beyond, for far away, over the
distant hills, was the village where she was born.
Then, with a sigh and a laugh, she sprang down the
steep back stairs to the kitchen where there was much
work to be done and no time to be wasted in thinking
of her home and her mother.

Another year passed, a long weary year for Betsy.

Mrs Dumbledore was getting old and cross. Her face was redder than ever and her temper got shorter each day. Betsy ran from pantry to dairy, from storeroom to larder, but she could not go fast enough for Mrs Dumbledore, who cuffed her and scolded her on all occasions.

It was the day for gingerbreads, and when Mrs Dumbledore looked into the iron spice-box where the ginger was kept, there was none. Everybody was most upset, for who can make gingerbreads without ginger, that hot spice which has a little fire in its heart?

Just then they heard a little quavering voice floating up from the streets, coming like a sweet breeze through the window of the palace kitchen.

It was the old spice woman, with her basket of scented fare on her arm. She had trudged in far countries over the seas, in those islands of golden fruit and silver flowers picking here and there, storing her basket ready for the cold lands where such things cannot grow. Her face was wrinkled as her own nutmegs, her arms were thin and dry as the spice she carried, but she lifted up her voice and sang in a shrill treble:

Nutmegs and Cinnamon,
Ginger and Caraway,
Spice for the Kitchen,
Buy, come buy.

'Betsy, take this crown and buy ginger from the old woman. Run quickly, run!' scolded Mrs Dumbledore, and Betsy hurried out of the kitchen, with her white cap awry, and her frilled apron tucked under her arm, with her little blue frock kilted round her, and her wooden shoes clop-clopping over the cobbled yard, past the fine sentry, through the great gates to the old spice woman, who was waiting in the street with her basket on her arm and love in her heart for the girl she remembered.

'What is your heart's desire to-day, my dear?' she asked, and she held out her spices with the clean cloth atop.

'A crown's worth of ginger for Mrs Dumbledore, if you please, Mistress Spice,' panted Betsy, and she curtsied and smiled as if the old dame were the Princess of the Spice Islands herself, but her lips were trembling and her eyes were sad.

'Take this to Mrs Dumbledore,' said the old spice woman, who noticed the girl's trouble, and she wrapped the ginger in a leaf. 'This is for yourself, a root of green ginger from the Land of Dragons. Keep it, for it may come in useful some day, my child.'

Betsy thanked her and curtsied again. Then clutching the ginger in both hands she ran back to Mrs Dumbledore in such a hurry that she lost one of her wooden shoes on the way, and Mrs Dumbledore scolded her more than ever. So she went upstairs, up the long steep stairs, to the little attic. She put her green ginger at the bottom of her trunk, and then leaned from her narrow window, with arms outstretched towards home, but she could not see anything at all for the tears which dropped from her eyes. So downstairs she ran again, and started to work.

Now the next year, as you may have guessed, the

old spice woman came again to the palace gates. She had travelled by blue water and green lands right round the world, seeking fresh spice and condiments. In all her travels she had never seen such a sweet maid as Betsy, for the old woman could look into people's hearts and read their secret thoughts. Her mind was stored with visions of scarlet and blue flowers, of glittering fruit, and bright birds, of mighty rivers and dark forests, and olive-skinned children who lived there, but the memory of Betsy was the best of all. She was a very old woman now, and she could sing only in a tiny voice, but the song came clear and true, like the voice of a bird, through the palace windows.

> *Nutmegs and Cinnamon,*
> *Ginger and Caraway,*
> *Spice for the Cottage,*
> *Buy, come buy.*

It had been a sad day for Betsy. Mrs Dumbledore had given her notice to leave, and she was to go home in disgrace, for who would hire a kitchen-maid who had been dismissed without a reference by the Queen's own cook?

For the last time she was helping Mrs Dumbledore to make cakes. Nothing was right. The palace cats had drunk the milk, the mice had nibbled the butter, and the spice-box, the leaden spice-box which had contained caraway seeds ever since anyone could remember, was empty. Mrs Dumbledore said Betsy had eaten them all. The cook was in a raging fury, and

Betsy was pale and anxious, for here was trouble even at the last moment.

Then they heard the fluting bird tones of the old spice woman out in the street, and the scent of the spices was in the air.

'Take this crown, and go quickly and buy caraway,' cried Mrs Dumbledore, giving the girl a push. 'Be quick. No dawdling. Let me have no more carelessness on your last morning.'

So Betsy ran out, and her little white cap fell off, showing her golden hair all bunched up underneath it, so bright that the red and gold sentry quite forgot his duty and stared after her as she ran clop-clopping past, with her hand outstretched and her pale pretty face eager to see the old woman again, as she walked up and down, with her basket on her arm and good fortune in her heart.

'And what is your wish to-day, my dear?' she asked, and she held out her basket which had nut leaves covering it.

'A crown's worth of caraway for Mrs Dumbledore, if you please, Mistress Spice,' said Betsy, and she curtsied and smiled at the old woman as if she were the Queen of Fairyland herself, but the curtsey was trembling, and the smile was only a flicker, and a tear rolled from each blue eye.

'Take this to Mrs Dumbledore,' said the old woman holding out a little box of caraway seeds. 'But keep these for yourself. You'll want them very soon now.' She gave the maiden a little packet wrapped up in one of the nut leaves, and Betsy put it in her pocket with many thanks. She wanted to throw her arms round the old spice woman and weep there, but she felt humble and shy. So, with the little brown box under her arm, she ran back across the courtyard, and as she passed the red and gold sentry he bowed and held out the white mob-cap which she had lost.

'My heart,' said he. 'I mean, my cap,' said he, and then he stammered: 'That is to say, your cap, my heart.'

Betsy curtsied, confused, and took her cap with a shy glance at the tall young man who looked as fine as the king himself. Then on she ran to Mrs Dumbledore with the caraway seeds, and her ears were boxed for her slowness in returning.

The ill-tempered cook made a hundred little caraway cakes for the royal tea-table, but even before they were out of the oven Betsy had gone upstairs for the last time, to put her packet of seeds in the trunk and to lay her clothes neatly over them. She gazed out of the window, the narrow window up in the tower, and far away on the white highroad she saw a tiny figure gliding along, the old spice woman with her basket on her arm and her staff in her hand. Yet she walked not as an old woman, but with the sprightly step of a young girl, as if her troubles were over and she had slipped back again into youth, possessing its joys without its sorrows, its riches without its poverty.

The tall sentry, who was off duty, carried Betsy's tin trunk down the two hundred stone stairs, and put

it in the carrier's cart, with never a word. Betsy rode
away from the palace, jogging behind the white horse,
home to the village where her poor mother dwelt.

Betsy had sent home every penny she could spare
during her life in the palace kitchen, and now, with
no money coming in, they had to live in extreme poverty. Nobody would hire a girl who had been turned
away by the Queen's own cook, even though she
could make angel cakes and queen cakes, saffron buns
and girdle-scones. So Betsy earned her living by gath-
ering blackberries, or by marketing the produce of
the little garden which surrounded the thatched cottage, the apples and plums and the bonny red roses
and striped gillyflowers.

One day she thought of the spices which still lay at
the bottom of the trunk in her bedroom. She brought
them downstairs and showed them to her mother.
They were green as grass, and not fit to put in a cake,
so she took them out to the garden and planted them
in the little grass plat where she sometimes sat with
her sewing in the evenings. She put them carefully
in the deep earth, and watered them from the rain-
tub, and she gave a thought and a sigh to the old spice
woman. Mistress Spice she had always called her, she
reminded herself, but nobody knew what was really
the name of the wandering magician with her basket
of treasures.

A few days later she was astonished to see them
sprouting, sending up little green-tasselled shoots,
which grew at such a rate that in a month four bushy
trees stood in the garden, with glossy leaves and ex-

quisite flowers. The pink and white and rose-
coloured blossoms scented the whole village, and
every one came to lean over the hedge and stare at
the strange foreign trees which had so miraculously
grown.

Meanwhile at the palace things were going badly.
The cakes were heavy as stone and badly made, for
there was no willing little kichen-maid to beat the
eggs till they were light as a feather, to froth the
cream, to sieve the flour. The spice-boxes of wood,
pewter, iron, and lead were empty. Mrs Dumbledore
listened for the old spice woman, but she never came.
The little song was no longer heard in the street, for
the spice woman had gone on the longest journey of
all.

The sentry in his red and gold uniform stamped
angrily up and down before the palace gates, for he
missed the sight of the merry little kitchen-maid who
was always too busy to glance at him. The Queen
complained, and the King sent Mrs Dumbledore
packing, so nobody had any cakes at all.

Then the sentry thought it was time to take action.
He marched out of the guardroom, and borrowed a
horse from the royal mews. He rode over hill and
through dale till he came to the village where Betsy
lived. There she was, in her blue frock and white
apron, standing on tiptoes, reaching up to her trees.
Her gold hair was plaited round her head, and her
blue eyes were fixed in wonder at the beauty of
the flowers which covered the branches, just as the
sentry's eyes were filled with amazement at the

comeliness of the young kitchen-maid in her mother's garden.

He tied the horse to the gate and went close to the hedge.

'My heart,' said he, and Betsy turned quickly round with a blush and a smile and a curtsey, and went to her side of the hedge.

'My heart,' said he again, but no other words would come. Then Betsy laughed softly to herself.

'It's you!' she cried. 'Welcome in to see my trees!'

She showed him the four wonders. On one grew bright nutmegs, and another had twigs of cinnamon, and a third roots of ginger, and the fourth the brown seeds of caraway, yet all four at the same time had flowers of radiant beauty and heavenly perfume.

'My heart,' stammered the sentry for the third time, 'Her Majesty wants spice cakes, but no one can make them now Mrs Dumbledore has gone, and the old spice woman never comes. The Queen's greatest desire is for spice cakes for the young princesses. If you will come back, just to make a batch of cakes for tea, it will cheer the palace and make everyone happy again.'

So Betsy filled a basket with nutmegs and cinnamon, ginger and caraway, and rode behind the sentry, clasping his waist with her arms as the horse slowly ambled along. On the way the sentry suddenly found his tongue, and he told the girl all he had been thinking about since she went away, and he hadn't finished his tale when they arrived. It was a lovely story and

Betsy's cheeks were red and her eyes bright as the fine
sentry lifted her down at the palace gates.

The Queen took the spices and put coins in the
basket instead, and then she filled the spice-boxes
with her own hand. She asked Betsy to return and
take the place of cross Mrs Dumbledore as chief cake-
maker, but Betsy said she had already promised to be
the red and gold sentry's wife. They were going to be
married without delay, and they would live in the cottage with Betsy's mother, and each day the sentry
would ride over the hills to guard the palace.

'Then I must get another cook,' sighed the Queen,
'but I will buy your spices, Betsy, for never have I
tasted better. They are as aromatic as those of the old
woman herself, and hers came straight from the
islands of magic, I believe.'

So Betsy returned to the cottage and watered her
four trees. In a few days the sentry came riding on the
bay mare, to take back a basket of spices and to see his
Betsy. They spent the afternoon sitting in the shade
of the trees, whose flowers and fruit hung over their
two heads bent close together.

As dusk fell there came a little shadowy old woman,
soft-stepping as a moth, singing like a distant night-
ingale and the song she sang was:

> *Nutmegs and Cinnamon,*
> *Ginger and Caraway,*
> *Spice for true lovers,*
> *Buy, come buy.*

She stopped in front of the two, and held out a shadowy basket. Betsy sprang from the sentry's arms and curtsied as she took it. She lifted the gossamer cover with trembling fingers, and the basket was full to the brim with Love. Before she could thank her the old spice woman vanished, and only a brown bird flew out of the garden and away to the starry sky.

The Girl who
Married a Pixie

A poor labourer once lived in a small thatched cottage on the edge of Dartmoor. There he took his wife when they were married and there all the children were born. Fourteen of them, and all as bonny as the little flowers that grow among the grasses! Their laughter and merriment kept his heart from failing, and gave strength to his hands, but he was hard pressed for money to buy them food, and many a day they went short. The prettiest of all the brood was the eldest, Polly, with her long golden hair and blue eyes. She helped her mother all day with never a frown or grumble, and carried the babies out to the moor, where she sat knitting as she watched over them. It was there the Pixie must have seen her.

One night it rained in torrents, and the wind beat on the cottage and blew wildly round the corners of the little building, screaming and crying as if it wanted to come in and join the children inside. The cottage was warm and cosy, for there was a red fire of wood, and the family sat round the hearth playing dominoes on the trestle board.

Suddenly there was a tap! tap! tap! at the door. The laughter of the children ceased, and the mother put her finger on her lips and listened. The father took a cudgel and went to see who it was, for in those days robbers walked on Dartmoor.

He opened the door a crack and looked out, but he could see nobody. Then something brushed past his legs, and in rode a Pixie, no bigger than a hand's span. His steed was a heather broom, and in his hand he carried a whip of rushes.

'Good evening to you,' said the little man, sweeping off his green hat with a fine bow, and then standing by his broom horse, holding it by its bridle.

'Good evening, sir,' replied the labourer, and the children stared with wide eyes, and even the baby forgot to whimper and chuckled at the funny little man in his fine clothes.

'Will you give me your eldest daughter to wed?' asked the Pixie, without more delay, as if he hadn't a moment to spare. 'I'll give you as much gold as you like.'

'Certainly not,' cried the labourer; and his wife said: 'I should think not, indeed. Let our Polly marry a Pixie? No! Never!' She put her arm round Polly's waist, and the children all ran round their sister and held tightly to her skirts.

The Pixie was quite prepared for this refusal, but he called aloud in a strange tongue and the door flew open. In came another Pixie bearing a pot of gold, all shining yellow as buttercups.

'All this for you, and many a pot like it, if you'll

give me your eldest daughter. I've watched her on the moors and I love her and would marry her.'

'No!' cried Polly's mother. 'Never! Upon my word, what are things coming to? Off you go, little man, and don't darken my doorway again.'

She flapped her apron at the two Pixies as if they had been hens and away they went, one dragging the gold, the other riding his steed of heather.

You may be sure the family talked of nothing else that night but the Pixies' visit, and they told one another that never would they let their dear Polly go. Then Polly got the supper of roast potatoes and goats' milk, and put the children to bed. She climbed in beside her sisters, and lay thinking of the Pixie. Nobody had asked her whether she wanted to marry him. Indeed only the baker's boy had ever asked to marry her, and her heart beat as she thought of this strange happening.

Then she heard her parents whispering together. 'If we had that gold we could buy our cottage, and the field and the orchard beyond, and live here, rich as rich, with apple trees and sheep and a cow,' her father murmured.

'I could buy new clothes for all the children, and give them food every day, so that they would grow up strong and well,' said the mother.

Then they both said: 'But to marry a Pixie! No! We won't let our darling Polly marry a Pixie! Not for all the riches in the world will we allow it.'

The next night it was even stormier, and the wind cried and howled round the house, shaking and bang-

ing the walls. The children sat with their parents, and they spoke of the fierceness of the gale. Suddenly there was a tap! tap! tap! at the door.

'The Pixie,' they all whispered, and the father went to the door and opened it a crack.

In rode the Pixie again, and the heather broom pranced and kicked and snorted.

'Good evening to you,' said the little man, and he swept off his hat politely and stood waiting in the middle of the floor.

'Good evening, sir,' replied the labourer, and the children all came round to watch, for they had no fear of the little man. 'Will you give me your eldest daughter to wed?' asked the Pixie, calmly, as if he had never asked such a thing before. 'I'll give you a saucepan that will never be empty.'

'Certainly not,' cried the labourer indignantly. 'I told you before, sir, that we can't part with Polly.'

The Pixie gave a whistle, shrill as a bird's call, and the door flew open. In came another Pixie bearing a saucepan, dark and streaked with green, an ancient pot of bronze.

The Pixie put it on the floor, and said something. Into the pan flew a cock pheasant, and sat there content.

He spoke again, and a piglet wriggled and squealed in the saucepan.

Again he spoke and a plum pudding all hot and sweet-smelling simmered there.

The children's eyes nearly popped out of their

heads and they shrieked with excitement as the Pixie held out the saucepan to their father.

'All this for you, and another pot like it, if you'll give me your eldest daughter. I've watched her on the hills, and I love her and would marry her.'

'Never! Never!' cried the parents, and away went the Pixies without another word.

Now the maiden's eyes had been fixed upon the Pixie, and she saw something she liked. His small wee face was kind, although it was wrinkled like a walnut. His smile was merry, and the glance he cast on her was full of love.

'Why shouldn't I marry him?' she said to herself. 'I was going to marry the baker's boy, but he whips his horse cruel hard, and he might whip me. The Pixie carried a whip, but he never used it to that broomstick nag of his. I think he'd be a better husband than the baker's boy.'

So when the Pixie came the third time, riding into the house on a wilder night than ever, carrying a musical box which would play every tune in the world, she up and spoke.

'Father and Mother dear! I've a mind to wed the Pixie,' said she. 'If he brings you the pot of gold, and the never-empty saucepan, and the musical box which will play every tune, then I will wed him.'

The Pixie clapped his little hands, and in came other Pixies with the gifts. The father and mother protested and wept, but Polly's mind was made up. She slipped into her bedroom, and made up her clothes in a bundle, her Sunday dress, her best shoes, her aprons, and she followed the little fellow out into the night.

'Climb up behind me, dear heart,' said the Pixie, and she sat on the heather broom, and put her thumbs on his slender strong waist.

Up they rose in the air, whirling through the wind over the dark moor till they came to the group of black rocks called 'Honey Bag Tor'. On the face of the greatest rock the Pixie knocked three times, and the side of the stone opened. The girl stared up at the sky and round at the cowering wild ponies sheltering by the tor, their eyes wide, their nostrils quivering, for they knew one of the little people was near them.

'Come along to your new home, Polly dear,' said the Pixie, and he tenderly took her hand and led her inside the darkness of the rock. Down and down they went to the great rooms, warmed by earth-heat, lighted by luminous stones decorated with flowers made out of gold and precious stones, the work of the little men. Pixies, you should know, have carved and cut the gems of the underworld for long ages, ever since man displaced them on the green earth and sent them to their own land, and they are skilful and clever beyond human knowledge.

In the vast hall many tables were spread for the wedding feast, and the young girl walked proudly down the room by the side of the little man to her seat.

'She's here! She's come at last! The human girl has come!' cried the Pixies and a thousand guests waved their hands and came swarming out of the many passages chattering in a strange tongue, and clambering to their tiny chairs.

There was honey in gold dishes, and Devonshire cream in crystal bowls. There was sweet bread made from the yellow wheat of the cornfields, and wine from the heather-bells. The girl Polly ate the good food and drank the scented heather-wine, for she was hungry after the wild ride across the moor.

'What a tale I'll have to tell them when I go home,' she thought. 'Won't Father be surprised! And Mother, too! My sisters and brothers will like to hear of this fine feast. Perhaps the Pixie will let me take some strawberries and peaches.'

In those warm lands deep in the earth grew fruits and flowers of tropical countries, and Polly tasted and enjoyed things she had never met before.

Then came an ancient Pixie, as old as the hills, with a beard sweeping the ground. He married her to her lover, and bound her finger with a ring of grasses.

Even as the old manikin spoke the words of wisdom over her, she grew smaller, till she was only as big as the Pixies themselves. Then she was taken to her room, a blue and silver bedroom, and the bed was covered with silk sheets and lambs' wool blankets. Hanging behind woven tapestries were dresses fine as cobwebs, and chests of jewels and clothes rich and rare, all made ready for the Pixie bride. Polly took off her country clothes, which were shrunken and queer like the withered leaves of last year. Her little bundle was not needed, her Sunday dress was a blue tattered

rag, and she looked at it in wonder. Already her
memory was changed. Once she had worn that dress,
and those old shoes and stockings. Somebody had
blessed her and kissed her, someone far away. She
put on the tiny linen nightgown laid out on her bed
ready for her, and brushed her shining hair. Then she
got into bed, and slept. How long she was asleep I
cannot tell you, but when she awoke she remembered
nothing of her past life.

The Pixie husband was kind and loving, and she
was happy with him. In time she bore him a son, and
then a daughter, and the little half-human children
had great beauty. They played in the rock's interior,
and ran shouting down the bright corridors deep in
the earth. But when the moon was full they came
through the stone door and rode their heather brooms
on the purple moorland, or they clung to the manes
of the Dartmoor ponies and were carried shrieking
and laughing, as they kicked their small heels against
the animals' necks, across the valleys and over the
hills of the moor. Polly had forgotten that outside
world, and even when she stepped on the heather, a
tiny creature in her green dress, no memory came of
the life she had once lived there.

When the two children were nine or ten years old
by Pixie reckoning, Polly suddenly remembered her
father and mother and the cottage where she was
born, and the reason she thought of them was this.
Her young children came running home dragging a
baby's slipper which they had found on the tor, dropped by some mother from her infant's foot. Polly

turned it over, wondering why it stirred some vague memory in her mind. Then she saw her own mother with the happy brood of children in the thatched cottage, and herself with the baby, sitting on the moor. The memory of home came flooding over her with such force she couldn't resist it. She went to her Pixie husband and said to him:

'My dear one, I have just remembered my home, the cottage where my mother and father live, and all the little ones. I remember the hearthstone, and the potatoes roasting in the open fire, and the sticks crackling in the chimney. Let me go and visit them.'

'Don't go, beloved,' implored the Pixie. 'This is your home. One can never retrace one's steps.'

'Oh let me go! I must tell them about my own children,' she cried, clutching his arm. 'I must kiss them all, for I love them.'

So he took her by the hand and led her out of the great door in the rock, and gave her a drink of the pale wine which she had tasted at her wedding feast. She grew tall once more, and she walked over the moorland tracks, past the great tors, walking many a mile, breathing the cold pure air, stepping so lightly over the heather that her feet scarcely bent the purple flowers. Sometimes she ran, and her long golden hair flew like wings behind her. Animals and birds had no fear of her, for she made no sound as she sped by.

At last she came to the little valley she knew so well, to the stream where she had paddled, and the rocks where she had nursed her sisters and brothers.

She turned the corner, and stopped bewildered. Where the cottage used to stand was a great house, with strange horseless carriages, black and shining as giant beetles, rolling in and out of a broad drive, hooting and shrieking like owls and night birds.

She stood very still, listening, staring, not daring to venture near. Then she saw an old man coming up the hill, carrying a basket of mushrooms, and she stepped over the grass on her bare feet, and held out her white arms to him.

'Please will you tell me where Primrose Cottage is? I thought it was here. I am sure it was here,' she asked, and her voice had the music of fairy people in it.

'I've never heard of it,' he replied slowly, staring at her long straight green dress, and the gold hair hanging like a cloak around her.

'But this is the place. I remember. There is the gate, and the field where I used to play. What is that house?'

'It's the Grand Hotel,' replied the old man. 'I've heard my grandfather say that once on a time there stood a cottage and garden there, but that was over a hundred years ago, and this hotel is for folk to come to the moor and get the fresh air.

'Where might ye be from?' he asked as the lady did not move.

She shook her head, and turned slowly away, and as he looked after her he saw that her white feet moved over the grass without leaving any prints, and the flowers remained upright as she passed.

'I've seen a Pixie, I'm certain sure,' said old George at the Inn that night. 'I could tell she was one of them by the colour of her long hair, and the way she walked, light as a fairy.'

'You should have held fast to her skirts, and not let her go till she gave you your wish,' said his friends, mocking him.

'Nay, she was crying, fit to break her heart. I felt mortal sorry for her,' he replied.

'Then she was no Pixie, for they feel neither sorrow nor pain,' said another.

'I tell ye, she was a Pixie, I'm certain sure, and she stood looking at the Hotel, and talking about some cottage or other.'

'There's a tale of a girl who lived there once, on the moor's edge. She went off with the Pixie folk, and was never heard of again. Clean disappeared off the face of the earth, they say, and her mother and father mourned all their lives, rich as they were. The children went away and lived over Exeter, but the parents looked for her always, and stayed here on the moor, waiting for her to come back.'

It was an ancient man in the corner who spoke, and some said by his queer ways he was a relation of that Pixie-led girl.

'Then I've seed her. That was who she was. She'd come back to find her home. Come back and everyone gone,' said old George, and he called for a pot of ale, and drank to try to forget the girl's grief.

At the stone doorway of Honey Bag Tor waited the green Pixie man. In his hand he had the cup of forgetfulness, for he knew that his wife would only find sorrow when she walked the moor again. Then he saw his dear one, wandering with her head bent, her step wavering and lost, as she fell in the bogs and stumbled over the rocks. Her tears were bringing back her mortality, and she felt all the griefs and troubles of mankind, nor could she find the way to the Pixie folk or remember the life she had led with them.

He ran to meet her, crying: 'Dear wife! Beloved Polly! How we have missed you! How we have longed for your return! The children are calling for you. Come, drink and forget again.'

'Nobody was there,' she sobbed. 'It was a hundred years ago they lived. All was changed, and the cottage gone, and they dead. A hundred years! How can it be when I am young and beautiful?'

'Time doesn't exist for the Pixie folk. We live outside it, and it has no power over us. Drink this, sweet wife. Drink and then come down to your home and your children.'

She drank deep of the draught in the crystal cup and forgetfulness entered her mind, and immortality caught her up. She became small in stature and gayhearted, and her sorrows slipped away from her.

Laughing gaily she ran down the rock's hidden ways to the little children and played with them through the enchanted days, and her husband loved her dearly. Yet sometimes a dim memory came to her, a faint remembrance of earth people, living their own human lives with their children. Then she took some small toy or treasure and threw it into the heather or laid it on the dark rocks, for the earth children to find.

So if you ever discover a tiny carved manikin made from a bone, or a pebble of gold, or a necklace of dew-drops like opals, you will know it is a gift from Polly, who was once a girl like you.

The Field that
Didn't Wish for Company

There was once a little field that was surely the loveliest in the world. It was so full of flowers that the bees
hummed, the birds sang, and the butterflies sipped
from morning till night, and when darkness came the
stars peered down to see the old earth's treasure-
house. It was tucked away in a corner between great
smooth meadows of mowing grass and rippling cornfields. These big fields with their rich crops were the
farmer's pride, the glory of his farm. Nobody tended
the little three-cornered croft, for the big fields kept
it hidden and when the corn grew high and the mowing grass was heavy with the faint purple bloom of its
bents and the crimson of sorrel, the secret little field
was quite forgotten and lost.

It was a jewelled brooch pinned on the earth's
bosom, holding her green shawl round her old shoulders. It was a garden sown with wild flower seeds,
prinked and petalled with every hue, kept for Old
Mother Nature herself to walk in and remember her
youth.

No footpath cut across it, no gate led into it, for the

ground was so uneven and rough that the cattle were not turned there to graze, nor the sheep to nibble.

It was confined on two sides by a tall straggling hedge of old trees, where twisty crab-apples and ancient hawthorns and prickly hollies grew close together, with here and there a great oak tree, whose rugged trunk was like stone. There was such a tangle of branches, such a web of intertwined boughs that scarcely a glimpse of the little flowery meadow came through the green. In and out of the latticed windows of thorn hopped the titmice, and from the trapeze of traveller's-joy the goldfinches swung.

The third side of the triangular field was a high wall, whose massive stones, grey with patches of lichen, were welded together with moss and stonecrop and bound with a thousand ferns and tufts of crimson robin-run-in-the-hedge. Under the wall grew tall foxgloves, with a hundred bells apiece. They stretched their long necks and peered over the wall, on the watch against enemies. In and out of their spotted throats went the bumble-bees, swinging the bells, singing loudly and triumphantly.

Every kind of flower grew in the little field. Its hillocks and hollows were painted with bright yellow pansies, with blue and white violets, and pale, sweet primroses and dancing, short-stemmed daffodils. On the rocky summits grew forget-me-nots, the colour of the sky at noon, and in the shadows by the stream was a drift of creamy meadowsweet, which scented the air with its vanilla fragrance.

In spring the delicate woodruff spread its white

frills under the trees, and the pale windflowers shook their little round heads in the west wind. Then the bluebells came like a pool of heavenly water, and on the edges the campion and ragged robin held up their bright faces.

In high summer the air was aromatic with wild thyme and rosemary and many a herb. Tiny flowers of milkwort covered the short grass with an embroidery of their own in tiny stitches of blue and magenta. Harebells rang their glass bells, and purple heather spread its own thick carpet over the black rocks and weatherbeaten stones.

When winter came the little field excelled itself. The trees were silver-white with hoar-frost crystals, and every blade of grass, every arching briar, was sprinkled with diamonds. The holly berries gleamed, the ivy beads hung in thick black bunches, and the little fir tree which grew in the rocks was a Christmas tree with its burden of sparkling playthings which shone there for the tree alone.

Although it was a secret field, its position was known to a few. A little boy and girl scrambled through a gap in the hedge, tearing their clothes and scratching their faces with the protecting briars and furze bushes.

'This is the best field of all,' they cried, as they leaped from the little black rocks and sipped with cupped hands from the spring. They picked the harebells and mauve scabious, they strung juicy bilberries on the long brown quaking grasses, and they filled their pockets with acorn cups and fairy toadstools. The jays flashed their wings at them, the robin whistled his little song from a wild-rose bush, the squirrel stared from behind a tree trunk and dropped a nutshell near them.

The children danced and sang. They called to the echo and mocked at the jay, but they didn't stay very long. Perhaps it was a thread of music in the breeze, or a whisper among the rocks, or the patter of unseen feet, or even that untamed echo which caught their voices and tossed them to and fro, changing them at its own will. The children gathered up their trophies of flowers and berries, and with quick backward glances they crawled through the twisted hedge to the farm fields beyond. Then they ran home, leaping and galloping as if to say, 'We are safe again after a great adventure.'

The poacher climbed the wall on moonlight nights and set his copper-wire snares among the short grasses, where the tracks of rabbits and hares were visible. But the snares were loosened when he returned, the wire was tangled, and if any creatures had been caught they had been set free again by an unknown hand.

So the time passed, and a year was only like a day in the heart of the wild little field.

One evening two lovers walked across the meadow and stood by the wall. In the dusk they could see the tall foxgloves peering over the top, and the scent of honeysuckle filled the starry air.

'Let us go in this croft. We haven't been here since we were children,' said the girl. 'Do you remember?'

'Of course I do,' replied the young man. He searched along the wall until he found two stones which made a rough step.

'Hah,' he cried. 'I once came here by myself, nutting and blackberrying. I got in this way.'

'But we scrambled through the hedge,' persisted the girl. 'Don't you remember?'

'We can't get through that impenetrable thicket now,' he laughed. 'You were such a thin little scrap, you could have got through a keyhole in those days.'

He helped her up the wall, and she stood poised like a white bird on the top. He climbed beside her, and then he sprang down to the secret field.

He held out his arms to her. 'Jump, jump,' he cried.

'See me fly,' she said, laughing, spreading out her white skirt like wings, and he caught her in his arms as she floated to the ground.

They laughed softly and walked with hands clasped through the tangle of flowers to the grove of trees.

'There are wild strawberries here,' said the girl, parting the leaves and discovering the scarlet fruit, and they popped the berries into each other's lips.

'There's the spring over there,' said the young man, and he curled his fingers to form a cup and held them in the singing fountain of spring water. Then he sipped from her little round palm and kissed her fingers and held them against his lips.

'The sweetest water in all the world,' said he, and drew the girl down beside him.

The water-mint and rushes were crushed beneath their feet. The air was deepest blue, and little gold clouds like cherubs sailed in the western sky. In the distance they could hear the voices of haymakers working late to get in the crops. The cuckoo called in the wild tangled hedge, and a white owl flew noiselessly over the corner of the little field.

They sat by the spring, listening to the sound of evening, watching the movement of grasses and leaves. Then they were aware of other sounds – little bells jingling, soft music playing near yet far away, thin whispers and low chuckles and murmurs.

'Hark! What is that? Do you hear something?' asked the girl, half rising.

'It's only the mice and hedgehogs enjoying themselves and the water running in the grass,' said the young man, but his voice was hushed because he was not quite certain.

'There it is again,' whispered the girl.

'Whatever it is, it won't harm us. Nothing could ever harm us,' said the young man.

So they stayed and evening drew down its veils. A drowsiness stole over the man. Perhaps it was the water-mint's strong scent and the murmur of the spring, but his head drooped and he fell asleep. When he awoke the girl had gone. He sprang up, shivering, for the air was cold as on a night of frost, and everything was different under the icy light of the moon.

He ran up and down the little three-cornered field seeking his lost love. The air was humming with little voices whispering and muttering in a way that frightened him. The tangle of grasses caught his feet and tripped him as he ran. He called, and the echo mocked. Night birds fluttered their wings in his face. The moon was like a white sickle in the sky cutting the fleecy clouds.

He stumbled over a little shoe by the wall, and

then he climbed into the field outside. On he went, calling, seeking, till he found the girl crouched beside a haycock, weeping to herself.

'Why did you go off like that?' he asked, angry at the trick she had played on him.

She told him that after he fell asleep she tried to wake him but couldn't. She shook him, but he did not answer. All around were glimmering shapes. The bushes were little old men; the trees were alive, staring at her, holding thick brown arms to her. The rocks seem to move over the grass, creeping nearer like black beasts. Even the little sweet voices of the spring sang more shrilly and called in human tones to her.

'Go away. Away. Away,' cried the voices, and the echo answered 'Away'.

'So I was frightened,' she continued, 'and I climbed the wall. Even as I got to the top something clutched my foot and seized my shoe. I thought I saw a white shadow, but it was only the owl. I jumped down and somehow managed to get to the hayfield, but I couldn't go any farther. I've been waiting for you to wake.'

'My dear, you've imagined it,' said he, soothing her.

'No,' she insisted. 'That little croft yonder doesn't like to be visited. I've heard my grand-dam say so. I had forgotten. The old people talk of it.'

They walked across the grass of the newly-cut hayfield towards the village, but when they reached the field gate they looked back for a moment at the tall thick hedge and the black stone wall which kept the little wild field hidden.

Was it fancy that they heard laughter coming from the stones and shrill piping music from the streams? Was it imagination, or did they really see faint shadowy hands upraised and a feathery cloud tossed like a ball to sink into the mist which wreathed that secret field?

So the little field was left to itself, and every year it grew wilder and more beautiful. Never were such pink roses on the bushes or golden coronets on the honeysuckle, never were such giant foxgloves or tall spikes of yellow mullein and speckled asphodel!

Other little children in their turn visited the field, and came back with tales of magic and wonder, and things which they hid in their hearts for fear of ridicule. Strangers came to the countryside, but still the little field remained wild and beautiful beyond compare.

One day a man walked that way, revisiting places he had known when he was young. He strode along the wall till he came to the hidden stepping-stones, then he climbed over and dropped to the ground. He wasn't so lithe and young as the last time he visited the field, when his companion had run away crying while he slept. He hadn't seen much of her after that night, for something had come between them. Then he had been offered work in the town, and he had gone away. What was her name? He had forgotten. Was it Jenny?

He had made money and married. It had been a good marriage for many things. They had travelled and seen the world. If he had stayed in the village he would have been poor all his life. Perhaps ...

He stumbled on something in the grass and picked up a wooden heel and part of a leather shoe. It was small as Cinderella's glass slipper, green with mildew, and tangled with wild thyme and strawberry runners. It brought no memory to him, and he tossed it away. He walked thoughtfully across the little field, peering here and there, looking at the stream and the fountain of the spring, measuring the field with his stride, muttering to himself.

'Yes, it will do. It's perfect. We shall be happy here perhaps. Yes. I could have a road made through the fields, and we can have the electricity plant put here, and an orchard here, and a rose garden over there, and the house shall stand on that knoll, with the stream running through the gardens making a natural cascade. Yes, Rosaline will approve, I think.'

The little field pricked up its pointed furry ears and rustled its grasses and pealed its silver bells. Its bright eyes peered, it shook its green hair and whispered with all its thousand tongues.

'Oh no!' said the little field. 'Not here. This is a wild little field. You can't come here.'

But the man heard nothing because he was deafened by all the noises of a city life and his senses were dulled.

'Yes. I'll have a house just here,' said the man, striking the ground with his walking-stick, and he paced up and down, treading the purple milkwort and the love-in-idleness, stamping upon the delicate petals of many a flower. 'I won't have it here in the hollow where it is damp from the stream, but on this little hill. I'll cut down the trees over yonder so that I can get a good view.'

He stood on tiptoe and looked at the blue hills and lavender woods in the far distance. 'I'll remove the hedge and have a garage over there, and a fine entrance with a lodge where the hawthorns grow.'

'Not here,' murmured the field. 'This is the field that likes to be alone.'

The man turned up his coat collar, for a sudden wind blew fiercely down his neck. He picked up the stick, which had fallen from his hand as if snatched by unseen fingers. Even as he touched the earth he felt a quiver of warm life move through his arm, for the ground was alive and breathing. He shrugged at his fancy and went to the spring. Stooping, he cupped his hand and sipped the cool clear water. Like a flash he remembered. It was there he had held a girl's hand in the stream, and as he drank he seemed to see her white dress float before him and her blue eyes look into his.

'Jenny! Jenny Wren! Jenny Wren!' he whispered, and the echo caught up the words and cried 'When? When?'

He went away and the field returned to its dreaming. A few weeks later he returned with a surveyor to measure the ground and an architect with plans. The turf was cut, the trees were hacked so that loads of bricks could be brought through the gap. Workmen came and scaffolding was erected; the house was slowly built.

And all the secret life of the field protested. The ants in their cities groaned together and lifted their little logs and carried them out like battering-rams. The worms raised their long bodies and spoke with thin reedy cries and writhed their way from under the house foundations. The spiders whirred their spinning-wheels and made long shrouds of silver-white. The beetles crept out with glittering, creaking armour and spied the vast mass of bricks which rose like a palace of darkness under the moon. But the field itself bided its time. It had lived for a thousand years and it could wait.

The furniture arrived in due time and the house was made ready. The first night the wind blew through every crack, seeking with its thin fingers to make little draughty holes. The rain beat down and the gales blew with such a flurry of wild voices that the man and his wife were alarmed.

'You can't stay here,' moaned the wind, and the little shrill voices piped and screamed, and invisible fingers tugged at doors and rattled windows and shook the walls. Inside and out the gale seemed to rage, so that the servants were driven from the bed-chambers to seek shelter downstairs.

The next day was balmy and warm, but now strange whisperings and murmurs filled the air. At night the mysterious wind came out of nowhere and blew its hurricane against the house.

The master, walking through the garden, looked ruefully at the broken plants and torn flowers. Then he noticed a young girl who was stooping over a bed of wild white violets which had been forgotten. Her small nose was close to the flowers, her blue cotton frock and white apron floated round her like a bell.

'Who are you?' he asked, staring at her rosy cheeks and her speedwell eyes.

'Please, sir, I'm Jenny, the new kitchenmaid,' said the girl. 'I came last night, sir. I lives at the village with my Aunt Betsy.'

'Ah, with your Aunt Betsy, do you?'

'Yes, sir.'

'And how will you like living here, Jenny Wren?'

'Jenny Borrow, sir. Well, sir, I don't know, sir. We none of us know yet, sir.'

'What do you mean, child?'

'This place, sir,' stammered Jenny. 'This field, sir. We used to call it "the field that likes to be alone".'

He stared at the pretty face looking up so innocently into his.

'Who calls it that?' he asked quietly. 'Tell me. Don't be afraid, my girl.'

'My mother said so,' stammered Jenny. 'She came here when she was little many a time. The field didn't like to be visited.'

'Your mother? Does she live in the village?'

'No sir. She died a while back. She told me about this field, how she was frightened one evening when she was here with one she loved, and she lost her shoe. Something snatched it from her foot and scared her.'

'Don't speak of these things to the other servants, Jenny,' he warned her. 'We don't want to frighten them too. You may go, Jenny Wren.' He turned abruptly away and went back to the house.

But the winds and the noises continued, and the servants complained of damp and cold and ghostly steps. They refused to stay and the house was shut up for the winter while the owners went abroad.

The field was very busy that winter. The wind shook the house to its foundations. Rains broke through the roof and frost split the walls. The silver spring which had been trained to run through the garden dived deep into the earth and disappeared. The magnificent rose trees which had been imported and planted in the good earth went wild in a single night. The flowers in the garden disappeared and the little wildings came back, scrambling across the beds and covering the ground with their own network. The seeds flew through keyholes and under doors. They sprouted and grew in the rooms. Traveller's-joy rushed up to the roof and climbed down the chimneys. Apple trees turned to crabs, brambles madly flung their cruel streamers over the paths, and grass forced its way under the paving stones and lifted the heavy slabs as if they were pebbles.

In a few months the field had done its work. The house was decayed beyond repair. One wild night of thunder and lightning it fell in ruins and the stones were covered with the quick-moving brambles. The field returned to its own wild beauty.

Then the little lost spring came out of the earth

again and dropped like a silver fountain into the hollow. Forget-me-nots grew where the house had stood and violets seeded in the crannies of the stones.

Sometimes a small white figure climbed the wall and came to the field. She cupped her hand, she sipped the water, and then she went away. The field was left alone till dusk. Then down came Night like an old nurse carrying stars for night-lights. She nodded her head as she looked at the field, and she pulled the white misty clothes over it.

'Go to sleep, my child,' she whispered, and the field slept.

The Shrew

Once upon a time there was a woman who was very unkind to her husband. She disagreed with every wish he expressed. If he said it was a nice day, she replied that it was horrible, but if he said it was a dull day she said it was beautiful. She contradicted every word of his.

Poor man, he did not know what to do to please her! One day he went for a walk in the woods and he met a little mouse.

'Oh! Little Mouse! How happy you must be!' said the man. 'Nobody to order you about, nobody to worry you so that you don't know a blade of grass from a barley stalk.'

The little mouse stopped eating. She fixed him with a beady eye and to his surprise she answered.

'Oh Man! How foolish you are! You have the sun, you have the rain and the flowers. You don't have to work hard to find the corn to eat. I wish I were you, Man. You are beautiful with your shaggy hair and your brown arms like the earth itself.'

'Now, I've never been called beautiful before,' thought the man, staring at the little mouse's fine silky fur.

'I will come and sweep your rooms and care for you, O Man,' said the mouse. 'I have long wanted to see a house where humans live.'

So that was why the little mouse went home with the man, nestled in his pocket. When the wife grumbled the mouse whispered words of encourage-

ment. When the wife threw a plate at the man, the
little mouse laughed and cheered.

'Don't dare laugh at me,' scolded the wife, and she
did not throw any more things at the man because
she thought he had enjoyed her anger.

But the little mouse, who slept in a corner of the
kitchen, got up at dawn the next day, and swept the
floor and washed it with scraps of rags. She polished
and cleaned, and made all bright and neat.

The man came down to make his wife a cup of tea,
and he was surprised at what he saw. Clean cups were
placed on the table, the teapot was shining, the tea-
leaves cleared away, and the fire was laid with neat
little sticks not much bigger than matches.

'Is it a fairy?' he asked. 'I used to believe in them
when I was a child, and I think one has been here.'

Then the little mouse leapt on the table and bowed
to him.

'Oh, it's you, my dear,' said he, stroking her fur. 'I
might have guessed, but I didn't know you were so
clever.'

But the wife grumbled more than ever. She
thought her husband had done the housework, so she
piled more labours upon him.

'You stupid man,' she cried. 'Why didn't you cook
extra for me?' she asked crossly, and she threw the
toast across the floor in her anger, as she saw her
husband quietly eating his breakfast without her.
'Why didn't you call me? You've been very quick
to-day.'

'It is a surprise for both of us,' he murmured, half laughing as he spied the little mouse under the table.

'Surprise,' echoed the wife. 'I'll surprise you. I'm going out to-day and you can look after yourself.'

She cooked her meal and then dressed in her best and left the house, calling: 'Now get the washing-up done and the kitchen cleaned, and the beds made and all tidied up before I return.'

'Very well, my dear,' said the man meekly. 'You know that I have to go to my own work, don't you, to earn money for both of us?'

'Bah,' cried the woman. 'Do as I tell you!' She flounced out and banged the door.

'Never mind,' whispered a small voice, as the little mouse came dancing out of the shadows. 'I can manage, I can get my friends to help. You go off, dear sir.'

The man was a market gardener, and he went to his garden to dig and sow and gather fruit and tend his crops.

When he came in for dinner, there was a white cloth laid and a good meal was ready.

The mouse had made a salad, using all the sweet green plants she could find in the little garden, leaves the man had never tasted before, but all mixed together so beautifully that it was a dish for a king.

'My little mouse, how did you learn to do this?' he asked, surprised.

'My mother taught me,' said the little mouse. 'She was a queen in our own country, and every queen is taught how to cook and manage a home.'

The mouse sat on the table and she helped the man to her dishes, bringing from her pocket a small silver spoon.

'This spoon belonged to my mother,' said the mouse. 'It is enchanted. Everything it touches gets a taste of delicious moonshine and magic.

'See,' she continued. 'I stir a glass of water and I can make wine. I stir a bowl of flour and currants and it makes a delicious cake.'

As she spoke she made the wine and a cake, and the man drank up every drop of the wine, but he took the cake in his pocket for his tea, after giving a piece to the little mouse.

All afternoon he worked at his market garden, and this time the little mouse went in his pocket. She gave him good advice about his plants, and she brought him seeds of chervil and basil and other herbs for him to sow.

'When these grow you can sell them,' said she. 'People like herbs and they will put them in their dull food to flavour the dishes.'

At last it was time to go home, and the man set off joyfully with the little mouse in his pocket.

His wife was there when he returned. She looked suspiciously at him.

'You managed to tidy up as well as go to work,' said she, sourly. 'I always knew you were lazy. But the house looks as if you have had somebody to help you. Who is it?'

'Wouldn't you like to know,' laughed the man and

the little mouse giggled in his pocket and tickled his fingers which were stroking her.

The woman was white with rage. She searched the house for some trace of the helper, but of course she found nothing. Not a footprint, or a finger mark. Then she found the little silver spoon, which the mouse had left in a cup on the dresser. She picked up the tiny bright object with a cry of excitement.

'Where has this come from?' she cried, and the man sprang to his feet and tried to take it from her.

'That's mine,' said he. 'Give it to me.'

'No, it's mine,' said the woman. 'I will sell it and get some money to buy a new dress, for you never give me anything.'

'Don't sell it,' pleaded the man. 'You know, my dear, you have all my money to do as you like with, and you can buy a dress with what I earned today. It was my lucky day.'

He brought a handful of money and put it on the table, and held out his hand for the spoon. But his wife would not let it go.

She made the tea, and stirred the teapot with the spoon, muttering to herself.

'May I shrivel and shrink to a cinder sooner than you shall have this spoon,' she muttered. Then she began to shrink, smaller and smaller. Soon she was down to a speck of a woman on the chair, but her face began to change too, her dress became fur, her eyes were tiny beads of light, and a small stumpy little shrew-mouse sat there.

'Oh dear me! What has happened?' she cried, and she leapt down and ran off to the woods, leaving the spoon behind her.

Then the man took the mouse from his pocket and put her on the table.

'How did you manage to do that magic on my wife?' he asked.

'It was the spoon, that can change man to his own character. Now your wife is a shrew-mouse, a fighting fierce little shrew, and she will find her match among the shrews in the fields and woods, for nobody will work for her.'

The little mouse took the silver spoon from the cup of tea and wiped it on her fur. Then she made a brew of her own, a scented brew of tansy and lavender and rosemary and ferns. She stirred the faintly smelling drink with her spoon and whispered some words over it which the man could not catch.

She grew taller and taller, her fur turned to delicate white skin, her hair was long and golden. She was a beautiful girl who sat there, in a dress of flower-petals.

'Oh, lovely creature,' said the man, 'will you marry me?'

'Yes, my dear. I loved you the moment I saw you walking so full of sorrow in the woods. Your wife has gone for ever, and you are free.'

So the two were married, and they lived happily for many years. The mouse was an excellent little wife, happy and eager and busy over her enjoyment with human affairs; the husband was enchanted with his pretty wife who knew so much, and could use her silver spoon to make magical banquets to surprise everyone who came to visit the happy couple. As for the shrew, she lived in the wood and sometimes one could see her, hurrying after insects and grain, struggling against starvation, fighting all the mice she met. Nobody would help her, her temper was so bad. When an owl ate her up everyone rejoiced.

The Snow Maiden

Far away in the icy north lived a great King and his beloved wife, and they ruled a kingdom which stretched across the North Pole, a land of snow and ice, with never a green leaf or a singing bird. The king was the Frost King, and his tall beautiful wife was the Ice Queen. They were old, they had ruled there for time unknown, but as they were immortal, age did not change them. They were white and cold as their vast domain.

They thought they had all they desired, for they loved one another, and that is a great thing, but each of them had a secret wish, a longing which seemed as if it could never be fulfilled.

'If only we had a child,' sighed the Queen, on the still nights when the radiant colours of the Aurora Borealis lighted up the sky, and the 'Merry Dancers' flickered across the snow in golden rays. 'If only we had a little girl, she would comfort us in our old age.'

'Yes,' replied the King, and he shut the crystal door of the snow palace, and drew the ice-bound bolts. 'I should like to see a child running along our glassy corridors, and playing in the empty rooms where only the winds live. She would bring cheer to us. She

would kindle a little joy in my heart, and the remembrance of youth, which helps one to endure all
things.'

They spoke of the days, aeons ago, when the Frost
King was young and he wooed the Ice Queen to be his
fair bride, in the early days when snow covered a
greater part of the world than it does now and the icy
glaciers reached across southern lands.

The North Wind howled round the corners of the
immense white palace, and shrieked down the chimneys, where dancing lights flashed with the resem-
blance of fire, yet giving no heat. He blew along the
snow cornices with their carved white flowers, and
puffed his cheeks at the great ice frescoes and pictures
on the walls. Ferns and forests of crystals were painted
there, and all the beauty of the tropical lands was
etched for the Ice Queen's enjoyment. The husband
and wife took no notice of the North Wind, or the
pictures which he changed every day. They sat on the
transparent blue-ice thrones, with their hands clasping each other's and their eyes gazing through open
windows at the beautiful colours of the changing sky
and the stars which peeped down at them.

The North Wind was strong and handsome, and
his eyes were as blue as night. He, too, thought it
would be pleasant to have a little princess, who would
listen to his songs and laugh at his jokes as he told his
adventures in the great world. He had travelled
widely, he knew far more of life than his master and
mistress, the Frost King and the Ice Queen, for he
blew over many another kingdom. He longed to have

a child in the palace, for then she would sit at his feet, and hear his tales of those foreign lands, where swallows build, and nightingales sing, and children run to school and chatter like a thousand brooks. Yes, he, too, wanted a child to come to the frozen north.

It was time to go, and he shook the ice-keys of the palace doors and flung them to his brother, the North-East Wind. Then he slipped his fur cap over his head, pushed his wild hair under the covering, and flew off, beating his strong wings like a mighty bird.

When he reached the warmer countries, he slackened his pace, moving more quietly over the green grass and the little foaming rivers. It wouldn't do to blow too hard, or the trees would be uprooted, and the wooden houses broken asunder. Even with his gentler flight, his breath was so cold the streams froze, the waterfalls became solid ice, and the raindrops on the overhanging eaves of the cottages were turned to icicles. People ran to shut their doors at his approach, to pile logs on the fire, and pull the curtains over the windows. The farm boys blew on their fingers to warm them and clapped their hands against their sides; the young girls wrapped shawls over their heads and hurried out of the wind's breath to shelter in the barns among the bales of hay.

Round and round the houses blew the North Wind, peeping through door-crannies and window-panes at cosy rooms where parents sat with their children, laughing and talking and feasting.

'Yes,' murmured the wind, and his voice howled as

he spoke. 'Yes, a little princess like one of those children would make the King and Queen very happy.'

'Ugh! What a draught,' cried the goodwives, and they stuffed the cracks with sacking, so that the wind could not get even a finger inside.

When night came, the mothers undressed their children and carried them up to bed, wrapped up in warm blankets. They would never let the North Wind bear away a precious child to that far land where the Frost King and the Ice Queen sat on their glassy thrones! The wind beat on the doors, and cried, demanding a princess, but nobody would give her child to him.

So he searched in many a country, but never could he find a suitable child to be the daughter of the icy north. Months passed, spring changed to summer, and the wind returned to the palace alone. Then came autumn and he started forth again, becoming wilder and rougher in his ways as winter approached.

In a little corner of England, high up among the green hills, was a small ivy-covered house, standing in an orchard. Snow fell, and the hills were whitened, so that sheep were lost in the drifts, and the shepherds struggled against the North Wind as they searched for them. Two children ran out into the snow and began to play.

'The orchard is much prettier than the fir wood,' cried the elder boy, and he looked up at the beautiful trees with their naked branches outlined with silver.

'Let us make a snowman,' said the other, and he

gathered the frozen snow in a rolling ball, and started
to build a man.

The elder brother, a fair-haired boy with large blue
eyes, and the long slender fingers of an artist, helped
him. Then he stopped.

'No, Paul. Make a snow-maiden. Everybody makes
a snowman. That's easy enough, but we'll make a
snow-girl.'

'I've never heard of a snow-girl,' pouted Paul. 'I've
never seen one. It's silly.'

'Then we'll be the first to make a snow-maiden,'
replied the other boy, with his eyes bright as he
imagined the beautiful girl he would mould from the
snow.

Rapidly they worked, pressing handfuls of snow together, the older boy moving swift delicate fingers
over the slim neck and small head of the little figure
he had made, the younger carrying the glittering
snow to his companion, following his instructions.
Gradually a snow-child appeared, with twisted bright
curls of snow upon its head, with wide vacant eyes
staring sightless, and curved unsmiling lips.

'How clever we are! Anyone can see this isn't a
snowman! It's just like a girl! I'll fetch an old hat
from mother to put on its head,' said Paul.

The boy artist shook his head.

'No. A hat would spoil her. Leave her alone, just
as she is.'

He was dissatisfied with his work. He stepped back
and surveyed the charming figure. She was wrong, her
body was a cloaked shaft, slender, and straight, yet it

lacked something. Her arms were not even there, they were unformed, hidden in the snow. Her face – Ah! he was pleased with her face! It had cheeks softly rounded, the forehead was noble, the ears like white shells. If only he could make the eyes look at him, the mouth smile, but that was impossible. He stooped and kissed the icy lips, and then he gave a little laugh.

'We will leave her, and come out to-morrow to look at her before breakfast. Now we'll put some holly and mistletoe on her dress.'

The young boy watched his brother place a berried sprig of holly in the snowy fold of the snow-girl's bosom. He fetched a piece of mistletoe from the bunch in the house and twisted it in the snowy curls.

'There! That's much better than a hat. Now she looks as if she were going to a party, like us,' said he, his face smiling and happy again, and the two boys ran off to the house, where in the excitements of Christmas they forgot their snow-maiden standing alone under the apple trees of the orchard.

The North Wind strode across the valley that night, blowing snow into whirling drifts, hiding all traces of roads and footpaths. He was weary with his search for a princess, he was disappointed with earth-children, who ran from him and banged their doors in his face. He feared he would never find a child who could live in the icy northern regions where he had his home.

As he stepped across the orchard, grumbling to himself with a voice of thunder, scowling like a black storm, glancing angrily at the closed doors and windows of the house, he saw the child. She was exquisite and pure as the newly-fallen snow, she stood under the trees, motionless, wistful, with eyes blank and lips unsmiling, yet curved as if the white-rose mouth would open and speak. Her head was slightly turned towards the house, whence came shouts of joy, and she seemed to be listening to one voice above others.

The North Wind stopped and touched her, but she did not shrink away. She was cold as himself, and his ice fingers on her cheeks gave her no tremors.

'An ice-maiden in truth,' he muttered excitedly. 'All she needs is the breath of life.'

He blew gently upon her, and a rosy bloom flushed her cheeks. Her snowy eyelids opened and blue eyes looked wonderingly around. Her arms moved under the snow cloak, and came out, slender and beautiful. She stretched them before her, as if calling someone. The curls of hair upon her head waved under his breath, her ringlets were tinged with gold.

'Come with me, child,' cried the North Wind, but she stared longingly at the house, and waved her hands to someone. In the lighted room, where the curtains were undrawn, a boy appeared, close to the window, looking out towards the orchard. He could just see the dim figure under the trees, and even as he looked it seemed to move towards him.

His hand was on the window latch, he opened the window and listened.

'Whatever are you doing,' said his mother. 'Quick! Shut the window. The North Wind will blow the candles out! Quick!'

'I thought I heard a voice,' said he, slowly. 'I thought I saw something move down in the orchard where I made the snow-girl.'

He turned back to the room. 'Mother, I made the most beautiful snow-girl to-day. To-morrow I'll show her to you. You will let me be a sculptor, when I grow up, won't you?'

His mother laughed, and stroked his head.

'We'll see,' said she.

The North Wind put his arms round the girl. 'Come with me, child,' said he. 'I have searched the world for you,' and together they rose in the night air, silent as snowflakes, for the wind was gentle as a dove with the child.

At the great palace he knocked three times, and each knock was like a clap of thunder. The Frost King came to draw the bolts, and the snow-maiden stood in the doorway.

'A miracle! A child for us!' he cried, leading her into the hall. 'Dear wife, here is a little daughter, come to live with us!' he told the Queen, and she dropped her frosted shawl and clasped the child to her heart.

'My dear one! My snow-maiden,' she murmured, kissing the rosy cheeks, and the snow-maiden kissed her back again, so that a soft colour came into the white face, and a look of youth glowed in the Queen's eyes.

From that day there was the greatest happiness in the palace, for the snow-maiden brought the ways of earth-children to the cold polar regions. She ran up and down the long ice-blue corridors, skimming like a swallow, and her reflection ran alongside, a little exquisite creature, clad in white furs, with pale gold curls clustered round her head. She flew, she skipped in a rope of twinkling ice, she danced. Sometimes the North Wind bore her in his arms, for she was light as air, and dropped her gently from the heights like a falling star back to earth.

The King was never sad, for he had a new interest in life. He made a harp with strings of spun ice, and the snow princess played and sang to her adopted parents. The songs came unbidden to her lips, songs of the stars and the great gold moon, of polar seas, and the iceberg caves.

There was one song which the Queen and King could not understand. It was about a boy, who stood in a lighted room, by a blazing burning fire, and he decked a dark-boughed tree with glittering fruit of glass. He came to the window and saw her. He stepped out into the cold and clasped her, but there her song ended. She knew no more, and when she finished she always sat silent and remote as if trying to remember something.

The North Wind knew the origin of her song, but he kept his secret, hoping she would forget. She was immortal as long as she lived with the Ice Queen and Frost King, and the wind used all his powers to bind her to the country of the snows.

He told her many stories at night when his work was done and other winds had taken his place. Then he sat by the pointed flames of the Aurora, which beat through the rooms of the ice palace, and spoke to the little princess sitting on a footstool of things he had seen in other lands, of green forests and wide yellow deserts, of ships like birds on the sea, and aeroplanes which he puffed with his breath. Every night he had a new tale to tell, sometimes of wild beasts, sometimes of eagles in the earth mountains. But the snow-maiden liked best his stories of children, little boys and girls, going to school, playing hide-and-seek, nursing their baby sisters.

Then she played hide-and-seek with the moon shadows, and the wraiths of snow which the North Wind blew for her out of the avalanches.

The Frost King ordered the winds to design a pleasure for her, and they made the loveliest garden, with apple trees, and tall lilies, and pavilions, all carved out of frozen snow. There was an arbour where she could sit under the snow trees, and round its eaves hung bells of ice which rang in the wind.

As she grew older she seemed to have forgotten her song, for it never came to her lips. She became very beautiful; her face was so fair that the South Wind and the West Wind came to visit her, to compare her with maidens they had seen in Greece and Egypt when the earth was young. They all agreed that there had never been beauty like hers before. Her foster mother's lovely face had become youthful again, her father had lost his age and was bright as a god. They worshipped her and gave her all she wanted.

One day the North Wind, seeking to please her, for he dearly loved the little ice-maiden, brought a present back with him. Clasped in his icy fingers, he carried a bunch of holly and mistletoe. No green things could grow in the ice regions, and he wished to show the princess something from the south lands. She took the scarlet berries, and the pearly mistletoe, and made a little crown of them to surprise her parents. When she placed them on her head, in a wreath of red and white berries, a sharp pain pierced her heart. She remembered something, a face out of a dream returned to her. She saw a boy, who pressed her snowy curls, and touched her cheeks with tender lingering fingers, warm, making her shiver with fear and joy. Then he stooped and kissed her lips of ice, sending love to her, and he put berries in her hair. It was true then, or was it a dream?

'Take me with you,' she implored the North Wind, when he wrapped his cloak about him and prepared to travel.

'No, Princess. This is your home. You can't go away,' said he. 'In the world is grief and fear. Here you are immortal, and know no sorrow.'

'If I am immortal, nothing can harm me,' said she. 'Take me with you to see those lands and people.'

Again he refused, and the King and the Queen, hearing the strange moaning cries of the North Wind, came out to see what was the matter.

'Do not leave us, daughter,' they said. 'Stay with us! You have given us new joy. We will give you all you desire, but do not go to that far land.'

The snow-maiden knelt and begged their forgiveness.

'I must go,' said she. 'There is one I want to find. I will bring him back with me, and then you will have a son and a daughter.'

'That cannot be,' they replied, sadly. 'No mortal can marry a snow-maiden.' But her prayers and pleadings touched them, and they decided to let her go.

'Only remember this. Keep away from the red blossom called Fire. We have never seen it, but this we know, it is death if you go near it,' they warned her.

The snow-maiden promised, and embraced her foster parents. Then holding the hands of the strong North Wind, she flew away, away, over the white stretches of snowy wastes, over the tossing green seas, across ice-bound mountains, to a gentle land, where streams ran foaming down the little hills, and sheep fed on the slopes. The North Wind took her to the orchard where once he had found her. He unloosed her arms, and, with a tender kiss, he left her.

As her feet touched the grass, snowdrops sprang up, and birds began to sing in the bare branches of the apple trees. She looked around her and laughed softly, for she remembered the little house across the path. She gathered a bunch of the snow-white flowers, and, holding them in her fingers, she went up the track to the door.

'Come in. Come in,' said an aged voice, as she knocked, and the Snow Princess entered. On the hearth blazed a ruddy fire which made her tremble and she drew back to the open door and waited there, staring round the room to find the boy she had once seen. By the side of the fire, with a hand stretched out to the blaze, crouched an old woman, haggard and lonely.

'Who are you? What do you want?' asked the old woman, startled by the girl's great beauty.

'I came to find the boy who once made a snow-maiden in the orchard there,' said the girl.

'Boy? There is no boy here. I don't know what you mean,' the old woman muttered.

'He made a snow-maiden,' said the girl again, and the heat from the fire burned and scorched her, so that she felt faint.

'You mean my son?' asked the old woman slowly. 'I remember something long ago when we were all happy. Yes, I remember.'

She turned round and faced the beautiful maiden, gazing intently at her.

'He made a snow-maiden when he was little, I remember well, for on Christmas morning when he looked for her, she was gone, and he wouldn't be comforted. He behaved as if she had been made of flesh and blood, instead of snow!'

The old woman was silent, thinking of past griefs, and the snow-maiden waited with a new pain hurting her heart.

'Yes, he was beside himself that day. He said she had been stolen, but there were no footprints in the snow, and anyway, who would take a thing of snow?'

'Who indeed?' whispered the snow-maiden.

'He never forgot her. He made a statue of her, and

called it the Snow-maiden, when he was older. It won him a gold medal and a scholarship to Rome.'

There was silence again. The old woman stared hard at the girl, and then rose slowly to her feet.

'The statue was like you,' she muttered, shivering. 'Who are you? Go away and leave me.' She sat down again by the fire, shaking her head. 'My wits are wandering. There is nobody there. I'm dreaming this.'

'Where is he now, your son?' asked the snow-maiden, in a soft voice, cold and sweet as a singing icicle.

'He is a famous man. I never see him now. He has children older than you. He has gone far away. He doesn't want me now.'

Then the snow-maiden knew that her immortality put her apart from mortals. She looked at the wrinkled aged woman, who had turned away sighing to the fire, dreaming of days long ago when her two children were with her. One alas, was dead, and the other lost to her.

The snow-maiden walked with steady steps across the room to the hearth where the flames danced frostily. She stood close to the fire and a terrible pain went through her, searing her body. She gave a wild cry and fell to the ground. At that instant the fierce wind blew into the house, shaking it to its foundations. The fire quivered, as the blast caught it and flung it aside. The snow-maiden was drawn up in the arms of the North Wind and carried half-fainting high in the blue sky, back to the land of Frost and Ice.

The North Wind flung open the door of the palace, and carried the princess to the Ice Queen and the Frost King. Slowly she opened her eyes, and saw bending over her the face of the North Wind and love was upon it. From her clenched hands fell the snowdrops which she had carried with her. She wondered where they had come from. No memory remained of earth.

Shortly afterwards she became the wife of the North Wind, to live for ever in the land of ice and snow. There she is Queen, for her foster-parents wished her to reign in their stead. In the ice-blue corridors run a troop of little children, wild as their father, strong as young giants, but their eyes are blue like their snow-mother's, and their voices are sweet as hers. Some people call them Zephyrs, when they fly over the lands with their father, the North Wind, and creep from under his cloak to play in the orchard, but that is wrong. They carry snow in their hands, and their strength is hidden. They are true sons of the North Wind, as anyone knows who sees them playing in the mountains.

Elizabeth, Betsy, Eliza
and Bess

On the steep stony hill above the village of Crumble
was a row of cottages. They were little old houses with
patches of stonecrop on the solid stone porches, and
tiny gardens and little paved yards. The people who
lived there thought they were lucky, for from the
kitchen windows they had a view over hill and dale to
the distant blue mountains. They were lucky too because they had a tap to themselves in the wall by the
roadside, and a deep stone drinking trough, as well as
an iron cup in the shape of a water-lily which dangled
from a chain. Every thirsty body could take a drink of
water, the ice-cold water which came from the spring
clear and fresh and sweet. Even the horses stopped on
their way uphill to the quarry village of Stoney Ash,
and drank from the trough. This made a feeling of
companionship with the outside world, a friendly
homelike bond with man and beast.

They were a small community to themselves, for
the leaden tap and the mossy water trough were the
meeting place for gossip and exchange of news. The
hamlet was called Farthings, and everybody in those
parts knew it. Even strangers leaned from their rattl-

ing gigs and smart carts to look at the four pretty cottages by the side of the road.

In the cottages lived a farm labourer, a cobbler, a smith, and a tailor, with their wives and children. The farm labourer was named Harry Shepherd. He milked the cows and drove the horses and minded the sheep at the farm higher up the hillside. The cobbler was named Tom Cobble for short, and he mended the heavy boots of all the men and women and children in the village of Crumble. He made strong boots for the farm men, and put iron tips and heels on the boots of the little boys. He was always busy patching and stitching. Jack Snout, the tailor, made the corduroy trousers, and leather coats, and the moleskin waistcoats. As for George Smith, his smithy was down the hill, and men from far and near brought their horses to his blacksmith shop to be shod.

Harry Shepherd, Tom Cobble, Jack Snout and George Smith went about their daily work on farm and in wooden shop and booth, and their wives stayed at home, for in each cottage there was a cradle, and in each cradle lay a baby girl.

The cradle in Harry Shepherd's house was made of straw, woven into a basket shape, with wheat ears at the top. Inside it lay little Bess, with her brown eyes and brown hair.

The cradle in Tom Cobble's house was made of oak, carved like a wooden shoe. Inside it lay little Elizabeth, with her gold hair and blue eyes.

The cradle in Jack Snout's cottage was of corduroy,

with stitchery round the hood and rockers of empty bobbins. Inside it lay little Betsy, with her fair hair and violet eyes.

The cradle in George Smith's house was made of iron, worked in fine tracery, with a hammered roof and curving rockers and beaten ironwork sides. Inside lay little Eliza, with her black eyes and raven hair.

The fathers doted upon their little daughters, and the mothers thought they were the prettiest children in the world.

One night, just as Harry Shepherd had taken off his boots ready to go to bed, and his wife had lighted the candle and turned back the hearthrug, there was a rat-a-tat-tat at the cottage door.

'Hark! Who's that? Who can it be at this time of night?' Harry asked his wife. 'See who it is, wife. I've taken off my boots.'

'Nay. I'm afeard,' said Molly Shepherd.

So Harry padded in his stockinged feet to the door and pulled back the wooden bolt and lifted the latch. On the doorstep stood a little man.

'Well? What can I do for you?' asked Harry, holding his candle near to look at the strange figure before him.

Without waiting to be invited the little man pushed his way under Harry's arm and walked with quick dancing step into the kitchen. He stepped on Harry's foot, and Harry started, for the little man had no weight at all.

The little fellow stared round the room with a

glance as quick as a mouse's. A sharp darting peep he gave, at the cradle of straw, at the lambing-can on the wall, and the shepherd's crook in the corner.

'What's your trade? A farm man? A shepherd? I can see your tools.'

'You see a lot, considering you've not been asked,' said Harry, slowly surveying the odd little man who bobbed and flitted like a shadow in the candle-light.

He was small, with pointed ears too large for his head, and bright eyes shining like stars. He was dressed in leather clothes, torn and jagged, patched and illfitting, stained with moss and damp. There were twigs in his beard, and irregular growths of orange lichen on his breeches.

'I'm a shepherd and cowman,' said Harry. 'And who may you be? Not of our parts I reckon?'

'No. I come from Far,' replied the little man. 'My name is Nameless.'

'Nameless?' echoed Harry Shepherd, scratching his head.

'I want you to make me a shepherd's plaid, out of the finest wool. There's a spinning-wheel in the corner yonder, and you and your wife shall show your powers. I will pay you well.'

'When do you want it?' asked Harry.

'In a week's time. I'll give you a bag of gold for it, if it's well and truly made.'

Then, with a hop and a skip he danced out of the room into the darkness.

'What do you think of that?' exclaimed the farm man to his wife.

'We can do it! A bag of gold! He's such a little man, we can spin it and weave it in a good plaid like your own wool plaid,' said Molly, and she picked up the cradle of straw and carried the baby upstairs.

That same night there was a rat-tat-tat at Tom Cobble's door, and Tom opened it himself. There on the doorstep was the little dwarf, eager and impatient to get inside. Before Tom could open his mouth to ask what he wanted, the tiny man edged his way round the corner into the room. He slipped across the stone floor and stood with his back to the fire, as if he owned the place.

'Here!' cried Tom. 'What do you want, Mister?'

The dwarf was peering round the room with quick eyes, glancing at the wooden cradle shaped like a shoe where the baby lay asleep, peeping at the cobbler's tools which lay on the bench.

'You're a cobbler, my good man. I see from your bits of leather and your last.'

'That's true,' said Tom, staring at him.

'Make me a pair of scarlet leather boots and I'll pay you well,' said the dwarf.

'That's a nice way to talk, with never a please,' grumbled Tom.

'I've never said please in my life,' chuckled the dwarf. He put his hand in his pocket and brought out a fistful of gold. He tossed a coin to the floor.

'A bag of this for your trouble,' said he. 'Boots of

the best, neatly made and sewn with small stitches, ready in a week's time.'

'Let me measure you,' said Tom Cobble, and he brought out his measuring rod.

The little man drew back in alarm.

'No! No!' He stamped so hard in his indignation that the cottage shook. The pots on the dresser rattled, and the cat flew under the settle. There, on the stone floor, was a clear-cut shape imprinted on the sandstone.

'You can make it from that,' said the dwarf, and without another word he leapt out of the door and was gone.

Next he called at Jack Snout's cottage. Jack was already in bed, but he put his head out of the window when he heard the tapping at the door.

'Let me in! Let me in! Work and gold,' cried the dwarf.

'Who is it?' asked Jack Snout. 'What's your name?'

'It's Noddy Nameless,' said the dwarf.

'I don't know that name,' answered Jack, but he came down and unbolted the door and the little man entered.

'You're a tailor,' said the dwarf. 'I can see by your big scissors and snippets of corduroy.'

'True,' said the tailor, shivering in his shirt.

'And you have a daughter,' said the dwarf, peering at the corduroy cradle, where a little frock and a doll lay.

'Right again,' said Jack Snout.

'I want you to make me a leather coat, and here are the buttons for it.'

He threw on the table half-a-dozen of those stones called haddocks' eyes, blue-green jewels.

'Make it as well as you can, and I will give you a bag of gold.'

'When will you want it?' asked Jack. 'I'm busy with orders.'

'In a week,' said the dwarf. 'I want it for my wedding.'

'Oh well, I think I might manage it for your wedding,' said Jack, who was plainly delighted at the order.

'In a week,' said the little man, and he skipped through the door.

'Wait a minute. I've not taken your measurements,' cried the tailor, but it was too late, the dwarf had disappeared.

'Then I shall have to guess,' said Jack. 'What a queer customer he was!'

The dwarf was already knocking at the cottage where the smith lived. George Smith was reading his newspaper and his wife was rocking the iron cradle when there came the tap at the door.

'Come in,' roared George, and he threw wide the door. He stared in astonishment when the little man skipped into the room.

'What do you want, little Hop O' My Thumb?' he asked.

'Two pairs of silver horseshoes, and here's the

silver,' said the dwarf, throwing a lump of metal on the floor.

'Horseshoes? Art thou crazed? What kind of a horse?'

'It's a little horse. I want four shoes each the size of a florin. I'll pay you well, with a bag of gold,' said the dwarf.

'When do you want them?' asked the smith, handling the lump of silver.

'In a week's time,' said the dwarf, and away he went, in a great hurry, for there was too much iron in the cottage for his liking.

So the four men worked at the strange orders which had come for them, and the wives talked together about the wedding of the little queer man.

At the end of the week the four men had their work ready for the dwarf. The cobbler had made a pair of high boots of scarlet leather, with wooden heels and square toes tipped with brass, and brass eyelet holes. The bootlaces were cornstalks plaited in a string, and tied with corn tassels. Very fine were those little scarlet boots.

The shepherd and his wife had made a grey plaid, with a fringe round the edge. It was warm and soft, for it was made from the best sheep's wool.

The tailor had made a leather coat with pockets at the side and full skirts for riding. He had pricked the front with his stiletto and starred it with tiny flowers. It had buttons of haddocks' eyes and scarlet stitchery.

The smith had made four little silver horse shoes, which surely would only fit a fairy horse, for no farm horse could wear such exquisite pieces of craftsman-ship.

In a week the dwarf returned, riding bareback on a white hare. He tied the hare to the hawthorn bush and took the four bags of gold which were slung over its back. He paid for the goods, and nodded his head with pleasure.

'Well made! I bid you all to my wedding,' said he.

'When will it be held, your worship?' asked the smith.

'In sixteen years. Meet me in sixteen years, and bring your pretty daughters with you,' said the dwarf.

'That's a long time to wait,' said the cobbler.

'My wife has to grow,' said the dwarf.

'And where will you be married?' asked the shep-herd.

'At Saint Mary's church on the hill?' asked the tailor, who was a sexton in his spare time.

'At the Methody chapel in the valley?' suggested the cobbler, who was a grave-digger when he had nothing else to do.

'At Windy Moor, in the Druid Circle,' said the dwarf. 'That's where I'm going to be married in six-teen years.'

'There's no church or chapel up there!' cried the shepherd.

'Yes, there is. It's an ancient one, and you'll see it when you meet me there, in the Druid Circle,' said the dwarf, and he slipped his arms in the new leather coat, and pulled on the scarlet boots and threw the plaid over his shoulder. Then he went to his white

hare, and fitted the silver shoes to its four feet. He
mounted its back and waved his hand and off he went
like a streak of light.

Sixteen years went by, and the babies in the cradles
grew into four lovely girls, tall and strong and straight
as young silver-birch trees. Although they were all
pretty, their characters were as different as possible.
Little Eliza who had lain in the cradle of iron was self-
willed and hard.

'If the little man marries me, and I am sure he is
coming for me, then I shall be his master,' said Eliza.
'I shall do what I like, and go where I like. There will

be so much money he will fill my purse every day, and I shall spend it.'

She tossed her head and shook her fist and danced a fandango, with her black hair streaming in the wind. Then off she went to her father's smithy, to watch the sparks fly and to hear again the tale of the

four silver horse shoes which the smith had made when she lay in the cradle.

Betsy, the tailor's daughter, who had lain in the cradle of corduroy, was a proud little girl. Ever since the bag of gold had dropped from the hand of the dwarf there had been a change in Betsy.

'If the dwarf marries me, as I am sure he will, I shall dress in scarlet silk with gold lacings. It will be solid gold of course, for he is very rich. I won't stay in this little place. My home shan't be called Farthings. No, it shall be Guinea-gold Hall.'

She whirled round in a dance, and her flaxen hair floated like a cloak of sunshine. She was very beautiful, and she knew it.

'No more corduroy for me! Silk and satin, and my father shall make my clothes for nothing,' she cried.

Elizabeth, the cobbler's daughter, who had lain in the cradle of wood, was a charming chatterbox.

'If the little man marries me, I shall tease him and mock at him, and laugh at his beard. I shall lead him such a dance that he will be glad to hide in a hole in the rocks. Ah!'

She clicked her little heels and flicked her fingers, and danced a country jig in her wooden shoes.

Brown-eyed Bess, who had slept in the cradle of straw, was a shy young girl, quiet and dreamy.

'If the little man marries me, and I hope he won't, I shall ask him to leave me at home. I don't want to leave the lambs in the spring, and the fields I know. I think Farthings is the loveliest place on earth. I couldn't bear to go away.'

'But there is no castle for a fairy man to live in,' said Elizabeth.

'And there is no fine company here,' said Betsy.

'I want electric light and water flowing through taps, hot and cold, and warm rooms and servants,' said Eliza.

'I can manage with candles and a water trough,' said Bess. 'I feel happier with these,'

'Oh, foolish Bess,' mocked pretty Elizabeth. 'You will change your mind when the gold pours down at your feet.'

So they laughed and joked, and even as they talked together they heard the clatter of little hooves and the dwarf rode up on his white hare.

'To-morrow! Meet me at the Druid Circle on Windy Moor,' he said. 'Four pretty maidens, and one of them is to be my bride – perhaps.'

Away he went, and the laughing girls looked at each other. Perhaps? What did he mean? He was certainly a handsome dwarf, not at all like the little man who had called sixteen years ago for plaid and jacket and boots. Over his shoulder the grey plaid hung, fresh as when it was woven, and the boots and jacket were bright and new.

'He has kept them in cotton-wool ready for his wedding,' laughed Elizabeth.

The next day they all walked up the long hill to Windy Moor. They were dressed in their Sunday clothes ready for the wedding. The cobbler wore his best coat and his leather boots, which were brushed so well one could see the sky in their surface. The shepherd wore his Sunday plaid, and carried his crook. The tailor was dressed in his suit of broadcloth, and on his shoes he had silver buckles. The smith had his coat of blue, and his breeches of nankin. The four men brought their music with them to play at the wedding. The shepherd had his pipe, the tailor a tinkling triangle, the cobbler a fiddle, and the smith a drum. The daughters looked beautiful in their starched white muslins, with pink and blue sashes, and little chip bonnets framing their young faces.

When they reached the black stones, called Druid Circle, they looked about them. Far below in the valley the smoke curled from cottage chimneys, and the fields diapered the grassy slopes. Hedges of mayblossom and fresh green beech woods stretched as far as they could see. On the hill where they stood the young leaves of heather and bilberry formed cushions, and emerald moss grew on the wet boggy ground. The Druid Circle, with its black rocks, lay like a charmed ring, and nobody ventured to step inside.

Suddenly the little man appeared, and the four girls smoothed their fluttering ribbons and held tightly to their prayer-books. The cobbler, the shepherd, the tailor and the smith stepped forward to greet the dwarf, but he stayed them with a proud quick gesture.

'Come along in! Leave your prayer-books on the moss and follow me,' he cried, and he leapt into the circle.

'Come inside this charmed ring,
And you shall dance at my wedding,' he chanted.

The girls dropped their prayer-books and they all trooped into the ring of black rocks.

'Music! Music!' called the dwarf.

Then the smith drummed, and the cobbler fiddled, and the shepherd piped, and the tailor tinkled his triangle, so that there was a gay melody in that upland air, but unseen bells rang louder, and unseen fiddles squeaked more shrilly.

'Take your partners for the wedding dance,' called the dwarf to the girls, and he danced alone while they spun round in their couples.

Then he chose Eliza, the daughter of the blacksmith, and danced round the ring with her. He went so fast, she felt as if she were flying as his arms held her. She heard the rattle of gold in his pockets, and she saw the gleam of gold dust on the heather under her feet, but there was no time to stop. Faster and faster they spun, and at last she dropped panting on the ground.

Next the dwarf flung his arm around Betsy, the daughter of the tailor, and he danced with her. She thought she saw the towers and pinnacles of Guinea-gold Hall; she looked up at the gilded roofs and tall chimneys, but they were only the sun-touched clouds. Her dreams fell away, the vision faded as the dwarf let her go and turned to another partner.

He chose young Elizabeth, the daughter of the cobbler. She glanced at the odd little man and her gay heart was filled with laughter. She twitched his beard, and mocked at him, and stamped on his toe with her little wooden shoes, so that he was glad to release her.

Finally he held out his hands to Bess, the daughter of the shepherd. There was a secret happiness on her bright face, and she smiled kindly at the dwarf, but her thoughts were not upon him. He spun her round the ring with him and he made up his mind that he had found his wife.

Then the dwarf began to sing.

> *Corduroy, iron, wood and straw,*
> *I like pretty Bess the best of the four.*
> *Straw, corduroy, wood from the tree,*
> *I'll marry young Bess, if so she'll take me.*

But Bess shook her little head, for she had seen her sweetheart, the sheep-shearer's boy, peeping at her from behind the rocks. They had never uttered a word of love, but in that moment she knew.

'No sir, thank you, I can't marry you,' said Bess to the dwarf.

'What! Corduroy, iron, wood and straw rejects gold?' cried the dwarf angrily.

> *Then Druid stones hold them all tight in a ring,*
> *For I won't take one for my wedding.*

He sprang from the circle and mounted his white hare. In a flash he was galloping over the moor to the blue mountains.

The cobbler, the tailor, the smith and the shepherd went on playing, for they couldn't stop, and the four girls kept dancing. Their feet ached, their heads were dizzy, but they couldn't escape from the enchanted ring where the dwarf had enticed them. Up came the sheep-shearer's boy, Gabriel, and he picked up the four prayer-books which lay on the flat altar stone. When he entered the magical ring with the prayer-books the spell was broken, the dancers sank down tired to the grass, and the four neighbours stopped their music.

So the wedding party returned to the hamlet of Farthings, and Elizabeth, Eliza and Betsy were angry at the trick the dwarf had played on them but Bess was glad, for now she knew that all her heart belonged to the boy who helped at sheep-shearing time.

The years went by, and there were many changes in the villages. Elizabeth the cobbler's charming daughter married the shoemaker in the big town. She went away to live in a fine shop, with two glass windows and rows of neat kid boots – button boots and lace boots, gentlemen's hunting boots and babies' slippers, all displayed on the glass shelves with mirrors behind. There were no clogs, or iron-tipped children's boots. Everything was very genteel, for there were even dancing slippers and glittering evening shoes with diamond buckles. Elizabeth had forgotten all about Farthings, and its little stone cottages, and its water trough.

Eliza the tailor's daughter had married very well, too. A master tailor had fallen in love with her pretty face, and they had a grand wedding, with four bridesmaids and organ music. Eliza lived in a new villa with hot and cold water and a white bathroom. She wore velvet on Sundays and silk every day. Eliza had risen very high in the world.

Betsy the smith's daughter, the handsomest of the four girls, married the rich old brewer. He loved his young wife, and perhaps she loved him. She certainly loved the money he gave her, and he was proud of her beauty.

As for little Bess, she married the young sheep-shearer, and she was the only one who hadn't done well in the eyes of the world, for she still lived at Farthings. There was no bathroom, only the spring at the door, and the trough where the horses stopped on their way up the hill to Stoney Ash and down the hill to Crumble. There were no parties, for the house was the smallest in Farthings. It had only two rooms, one upstairs and one downstairs, but the cottage was snug and warm, with thick curtains over the windows and a wood fire flickering brightly on the hearth. Bess's husband, Gabriel, always brought a load home from the woods. At night he sat with Bess, and in the straw cradle on the floor lay their little daughter, Elspeth.

One night when Elspeth was nine or ten years old, the door was pushed open. Elspeth lay fast asleep in the downstair room, in the bed which fitted in the wall. The moon sent its bright beams over her brown hair, and patterned the whitewashed walls with bars of shadow. The fire was low, with a guard round it, for Bess had gone out for a few minutes to visit her mother and father. Into the kitchen peeped a small

wayfaring dwarf, lonely and lost. He had walked half
across the world, looking for comfort and happiness.
Everyone was too rich, or too solemn, or too grand, or
too poor to take any notice of a little dwarf. It was our
own little dwarf, forsaken and deserted. He had mis-
laid his caves of gold, he had lost his hoards of gems,
he had thrown away his money, and he had forgotten
the art of magic. He was no longer proud and bold.
All he wanted was a little love and a little homeliness,
and he couldn't find it. He remembered once visiting
Farthings, and the girl who had danced with him. He
was shabby, his scarlet coat was in rags, the leather
boots were worn to shreds, and the white hare who
wore the silver horse shoes had run away.

Although he was a lonely little dwarf, he had still a
spirit of gaiety in his heart. Life might have a surprise
for him, as he had given life many surprises. So he
crept through the open door and came up to the fire.
There was a smell of hot roast potatoes, and under
the logs of wood some brown potatoes were cooking
in their clean-scrubbed jackets. On a bench was a
bowl of milk and a pat of butter. Just the supper he
loved! Once he would have gobbled it up without a
thought but now he hesitated and waited, crouched
on the hearth.

'Have some supper, little man,' said a clear young
voice, and the dwarf looked up to see the little girl
watching him.

'I'm getting slow, for you to spy me first,' said he,
gloomily. 'Once I was a nimble-witted somebody, and
now I am a nobody.'

'Who are you?' asked the girl.

'My name is Nameless,' said the dwarf slowly.

'And mine is Elspeth, and my mother's is Bess, and my father's is Gabriel Plow. My grandfather told me a tale of a little man who came to his house and asked for a plaid. Was it you?'

'It was indeed, and this is the plaid,' said Nameless, drawing the rough old woollen plaid from his shoulders and wrapping it round the child.

So they sat and talked, and the dwarf ate the good food, the floury potatoes, and the sweet creamy milk. Elspeth fetched the pewter salt-cellar from the cupboard, and they both dipped their potatoes into it, and laughed together in the firelight. Then back to bed crept the girl, and the mother returned and later the father, but nobody saw the little dwarf who lay curled up in the stick basket under the flounce of the settle.

In the night he arose and tidied the hearth, and polished the brass pans, and cleaned the boots. As he worked he began to whistle, very softly, joyfully, for his old magic was returning to him. He felt young again, unfrozen, and merry. He skipped round the room like a mouse, and from the bed in the wall a head of tousled brown hair was raised and two bright eyes regarded him.

'You are really the little man who came to my grandfather and danced with my mother?' asked Elspeth.

'I am the same wee fellow,' chuckled the dwarf. 'Humble now and poor, but the same.'

'Will you stay with us always? Don't go away this time,' implored Elspeth.

'I'll stay with you till the end of time. I'll be your faithful slave and friend for ever and ever,' vowed the little dwarf.

'Thank you. Oh, thank you, Nameless,' sighed the girl, and she lay down and shut her eyes.

So in that cottage lived the dwarf, and he cared for the family and cherished them all their days, giving them joys unknown to others, and they bestowed upon him human love, which is the greatest gift of all.

One-Strand River

Once there was a shepherd boy who minded his flock on the hills above a wild river valley. One of the sheep strayed and he went after it, across the rocky slopes. He folded the rest of the flock before he started, to keep them safe, and he took his dog with him as he ran down the heather, calling to the lost ewe.

At the bottom of the valley flowed a deep river and by its side, grazing in the thick grass, was the lost sheep. He was so glad to find it, he gave it only a little scolding and sent it back under the guidance of his trusty dog. He flung himself down in the shadow of a rock to rest for a few minutes before he returned up the long craggy hillside.

He lay dreaming of the beautiful goose-girl who had lately come to the farm to work. She was so quiet, so silent, he had never heard her voice, but he was filled with love for her.

As he lay there by the side of the deep mountain river, he saw the goose-girl coming along a narrow track with the flock of geese. He kept very still and waited in the rock's shadow. She was poorly dressed, her feet were bare, and her hands torn and scarred by the briars, but her face was very beautiful, and her long fair hair was the palest gold.

She came along by the river towards him, unaware that he lay watching her. When she was close to him he could see that there were tears in her eyes, and her shoulders were shaking with sobs. He was about to spring to his feet and go to comfort her, when she stopped and stretched out her arms to the water. Then he heard her speak for the first time:

> *Grey goose and gander,*
> *Waft your wings together,*
> *And carry the King's daughter*
> *Over the one-strand river.*

From the flock came a grey goose and gander. They locked their wings to form a hammock, and the goose-girl seated herself upon it. Over the wild river they flew, high in the air, with the girl resting in their grey feathers. Behind them flew some of the geese. The boy could see them settle in the meadow on the far side.

The shepherd boy ran down to the rocky bed of the river. The water ran deep and swift, but he threw himself in, swimming against the current, caught in the swirling water, then struggling in the treacherous waves which seemed as if they would suck him under. For a long time he fought the river, but at last he was swept into a pool and he struggled to the opposite bank. He climbed up the rocks and sank exhausted in

the meadow grass. There grew asphodel, lilies of the valley, and the pearly-white grass of Parnassus.

In the distance he saw the goose-girl, with her grey goose and gander, walking with her flock. He started after her, but he got no nearer. He called 'Goose-girl, goose-girl, wait for me,' but she did not turn her head. His voice was carried back to him, so that he heard his words echoing over and over.

'Goose-girl, goose-girl, wait for me, for me,' cried the blue hills, mockingly.

There she went, with her white feet moving un-hurriedly over the flowers, and her bright hair float-

ing in the wind, and the flock of geese keeping step with her. Then she disappeared over the crest of a hill.

When he had climbed the steep slope of juniper and myrtle bushes, he looked down the gap to the next valley. Far away he saw another river, winding like a blue and white rope, and beyond it were the mountains.

The girl and her flock of geese reached the water's edge, and there they stayed while the shepherd boy got nearer. He called, but she took no notice. Again she held out her arms to the water and he could hear her song:

> *Grey goose and gander,*
> *Waft your wings together,*
> *And carry the King's daughter*
> *Over the two-strand river.*

The grey goose and gander came from the flock and locked their wings together. The girl rode in the feathered cradle over the water, and below them the blue and white streams sparkled like sapphire and diamond. The flock of geese followed after.

The shepherd boy ran down the hills and reached the river. There he found a slender boat fastened to the rocks. He climbed in and rowed after the girl, but the blue stream took him one way, and the white stream the opposite. He was carried up the river and down again for so long that time ceased to exist for him.

'I shall never reach the shore,' he thought. 'I shall be here on this blue and white river for Eternity.'

At last he gave up struggling and let the boat drift. It turned at right angles to the current and went straight to the land.

In the dim light he could see the flock of geese asleep with the girl among them, and the grey gander keeping guard. He walked towards them, but try as he would, he could not keep his eyes open, and he dropped down and slept.

When he awoke he saw the goose-girl and her flock walking slowly across the fields. The flock was feeding as it went and the girl was singing. In front of them was a great mountain and the shepherd boy was sure he would catch her as she climbed the precipitous rocks. He followed swiftly, and he was very near, for the goose-girl seemed to be waiting for him.

He called 'Goose-girl, goose-girl, stay for me,' but she did not turn her head. Instead she held out her arms to the great mountain before her and sang in her strange lovely voice:

> Grey goose and gander,
> Waft your wings together,
> Carry the King's daughter
> Over the desperate mountain.

The two great birds came from the flock and linked their wings together. She climbed upon them and was taken high in the air over the rugged mountain.

Then the shepherd boy was nearly defeated. He could not return over the two rivers, and the mountain before him seemed impassable. He was filled with longing to speak to the beautiful girl who said she was a king's daughter, and to hear her story. He took up his crook and set off, walking for many a day, going north by the stars, for the goose and gander seemed to be flying to northern lands. He lived on berries and roots, and when he came to the high mountain where the trees ceased, he would have died except for the plants that grew there.

At last he crossed the range and began the descent into the valley. Below him lay a town, fair and golden in the sunlight. He walked boldly down the heather slopes, eager to find the lovely creature whom he had followed so far.

In a croft under the high stone walls of the town was the flock of geese, and he ran with swift feet towards it. There was no goose-girl with them, so he waited there with his crook and took care of them. At night he was wondering where to take them, when the big grey goose and gander marched up the hill to a green cave hidden among the rocks. The geese followed, and the shepherd boy with them.

The grey goose and gander tapped at the door and entered with the flock. Then the shepherd boy crept softly after. By the side of the fire sat the goose-girl.

She sprang up in alarm when she saw the shepherd boy.

'Nay, be not afeard of me. Don't you remember me?' he asked. 'I've followed you over many a mile of land and river.'

'Did you see me cross the one-strand river?' she asked.

'Yes, I saw the goose and gander twine their wings together like a basket and carry you over,' said he.

'And the two-strand river, and the desperate mountain?' she asked.

'I saw it all,' said he.

'And did you hear my name?' she asked.

'You said you were a king's daughter, but I thought that couldn't be, for princesses don't mind geese, except in fairy tales.'

'Nevertheless, it is true. I am the daughter of a king,' she said, softly, and she took his outstretched hand. 'I will tell you all.'

She sat with him at the door of the cave, and the

geese pressed closely around them to listen. This is the tale she told him:

'I was born in the town you see below us, in the white palace on the opposite hillside. There I was the happiest child, with no cares. One day, a dark king came to the palace, and he carried my mother and father away. They said he was the King of Shadows, and my parents had been taken to his land. They said that he wanted me, too.

'Then I fled, and he couldn't find me. I kept in the bright sunlight, for I thought that it was in the darkness that he had power. At last I ran away from my own land, and after many adventures I arrived in a far country. I took with me the flock of geese which I loved. I became the goose-girl at a farm, and I looked after my own flock and the farmer's. I told nobody who I was or where I had come from. I was dressed in rags, torn and dirty. It was better so. I slept in a chamber over the goose-house, and I ate my meals at a little table to myself, away from the rest of the family. I was too poor to be accepted by them.'

'And that was where I saw you,' said the shepherd boy, eagerly.

'Yes, you were the only one who was kind to me, but I kept out of your way, for I didn't wish to speak, lest the Shadow King should discover me. Always I kept to the light.'

'I wish you had let me talk to you. You never spoke,' said the boy.

'One evening, in bright moonlight, I heard a wolf among the geese, and I ran to rescue them. I was go-

ing back to the farm when I thought I saw a great
shadow hovering over me. I escaped into my chamber, but from that time I never felt safe, and I was
haunted by fears. I heard my geese talking together,
telling one another they could save me. The grey
goose and gander said they would carry me over dif-
ficult places. The others said they would go wherever
I went, so I determined to escape again, and to come
home.

'The shadow is here, still seeking for me. I dare not
venture to the palace, so I have come to this cave in
the rocks, where I played when I was a child. Here I
have hidden, and the geese have gone out by themselves each day and brought me milk, and fruit from
the orchards.'

'Let us go to the palace together,' said the shepherd
boy. 'I'll take care of you. That Shadow King won't
dare to touch you when I am near.'

She looked up at his bright eyes. 'Yes,' said she, 'I'll
go anywhere with you, even to the end of the world.'

'Perhaps we're there now,' he smiled down at her.

So the next day they set off down the mountain
slopes to the white town and the glittering palace.
The girl was eager to show the shepherd boy the
places she knew so well – the green orchards, the
gardens of flowers, the fountains and the glades. She
spoke of the goldsmith's shop and the forge where her
horse was shod, and the printing press and the puppet
show.

Then her laughter stopped, and a puzzled look
came to her eyes.

'It's all changed,' she whispered. 'These are different people, and the town is altered. The forge, the goldsmiths, the printing press have all gone. And the houses are different too. I don't remember this.'

'You've been away a long time,' the shepherd boy reminded her.

'It doesn't seem long,' said she.

Together they went to the palace, but as they were poorly dressed, they went by back ways, among the servants. The shepherd boy stopped a drover and questioned him, but the man went on talking to a companion by his side, and took no notice.

The girl walked up to a cottage in the park and knocked on the door. She tapped at the little window in its honeysuckle bower.

'Here lives an old woman who will remember me and tell me all I want to know,' she said.

Nobody came, nobody answered the knocking, but after a few minutes, the door opened and a young woman stepped out. She passed by the shepherd boy and the princess without seeing them, and went on her way.

The door was left open and the princess entered the little house.

'She may be within,' she explained. 'I always used to go in without knocking. She was my old nurse, and she loved me to visit her.'

In the room a man and an ancient woman sat talking.

'It's a hundred years since my grandmother died,'

said the woman. 'She remembered the princess and
the king. My grandmother never got over the death
of the princess.'

'What was the princess like?' asked the man.

'A lovely young girl, they said. There was a strange
happening. After the king and queen died, a dark
shadow passed over and took her away.'

'No,' said the girl, stepping forward. 'No, I escaped.
I am here!'

They took no more notice than if she too had been
a shade.

'The king died first and she disappeared, did you
say?' asked the man.

'I am here,' repeated the princess.

'Yes, a hundred years ago,' said the woman.

The princess took the shepherd boy's hand and ran
out of the house.

'It isn't true,' she wept. 'I am here. Say I am here.'

'Yes, sweetheart, you are here and I am with you,'
said the shepherd boy. 'They must be crazed.'

Together they went up the little hill to the palace,
and through the doors. Nobody stopped them as they
wandered through the rooms. It was a museum of
lovely things, with porters guarding glass cases holding the jewels and dresses of the little princess. Her
toys were set out, her puppet-show, her sampler and
workbox.

She wept softly, and the shepherd boy put his arm
around her and drew her to the golden throne. It was
roped off from the crowd of people who wandered

through the palace rooms, staring at the relics of past days. They sat there together, on the velvet seats, and he comforted her and kissed her, but nobody spoke to them or looked at them resting there.

'I won't stay here any longer. Let us go to the gardens, the fountains, to the roses. Surely they are the same,' she cried, springing to her feet and running away.

She led him down the wide staircase and out of the great door. They went along the stone terraces to the fountains and sat on the broad rim watching the play of the waters. That was unchanged from other days. The sun beat down upon them and made a rainbow in the falling spray. Robins and bluetits came to their feet and flew upon their outstretched hands. Flowers bloomed and tossed their petals over them.

Then they were aware of somebody coming towards them, looking at them, and seeing them without the vacant gaze of the people. It was a tall dark man, cloaked in black. His eyes were deep-set, and there was kindness in their glance. He came swiftly towards them, casting no shadow, making no sound. The girl leapt to her feet with a cry. 'The King, the Shadow King.'

'So you have come at last, my child,' he said quietly. 'Why did you try to escape me?'

'The Shadow King,' she whispered.

'Yes, the Shadow King. Your father has been waiting for you, and your mother is here. They will welcome this sweetheart of yours who crossed the one-strand river, and the two-strand river, and the desperate mountain for love of you.'

'The one-strand river,' echoed the princess.

'Yes. Some call it the river of death, but others say it is the river of life,' replied the dark king, smiling. He turned to the palace, where many people were moving.

'See, they are coming to welcome you,' he said.

Down the palace steps came the king and queen with their arms held out, and behind them was a crowd of happy, jostling people.

The little princess ran to meet them.

'Mother! Father!' she cried. 'Oh, where have you been? It is so long since I saw you. Oh, Mother, Father, how I have missed you!'

'We have been here all the time, dear child,' they answered, embracing her. 'We only went down to the one-strand river, to bathe in its waters, and when we returned you had gone.'

'Mother, Father. Here is the one I love. He has followed me through the world. For my sake, love him too, dear Mother and Father.'

'We do love him, child. We welcome him as a son.'

The moon was shining in the East and the sun was burning in the West. The stars peeped down in the daylight, and music came out of the sky where the planets swung. A thousand people swayed over the grass, dancing to the fountain, rejoicing that the little princess had come home to the palace with her husband the shepherd boy.

Far, far away, and long, long ago, the sheep returned to the farm without their shepherd, and the geese returned without their goose-girl. Only the flock of wild geese, with the grey goose and gander, had crossed the one-strand river, to the country from which nobody ever returns.

The Grandfather-Clock
and the Cuckoo-Clock

One day the Grandfather rubbed his eyes, yawned and climbed out of the grandfather-clock in the hall, where he had lived for two hundred years. The clock stopped ticking, the weights ran down, and there was silence.

He tripped lightly across the hall, drawing his old cloak around his shoulders, and pressing his tall hat on his head, he tapped at the tiny door in the carved wooden cuckoo-clock, hanging on the wall. The painted Cuckoo looked out, and then fluttered down to join him.

They slipped through the open window, and walked across the garden where the mignonette and poppies were blooming. Old Grandfather picked a sprig of lad's-love, which he stuck in his hat, and the Cuckoo flew up to his shoulder.

What a picture they made as they stood under the apple trees, sniffing at the sweet scents, listening to the birds, drinking the fragrant air! But no one saw them there.

'Let's go down the lane,' said the Grandfather, 'and see how the haymakers are getting on. I can smell the hay, and it's a hundred years since I was out.'

So down the lane they went, light as thistle-down, making no sound except their laughter.

In the meadows were babies tumbling over in the hay, and the haymakers tossed and raked the grass. A hay-cart, drawn by a great mare, came lumbering through the gate, laden with a heavy load.

Grandfather climbed up on the gate, and sat there swinging his legs, watching the men at work. But the little Cuckoo flew to a tree, and cuckooed twelve times.

'Oh ho!' cried Grandfather. 'Is it as late as that?' and he struck twelve with his deep ringing voice.

The haymakers put down their forks and rakes, and walked off to the hedge where their dinners lay in brown baskets under the dock leaves. The mare was set free from her load, and she whinnied her thanks to the strange pair.

Down jumped Grandfather and the Cuckoo, and they walked across the fields to the village school. They peeped through the open windows at the hot little children, sucking their pencils, frowning, wriggling, shuffling, as they struggled with their lessons.

'They ought to be out in the hay-field,' whispered the Grandfather to the Cuckoo.

So the Cuckoo called twelve times, and the Grandfather struck. All the children shut their books, and prepared to go home.

'My clock must be very slow!' murmured the teacher to herself. 'I had no idea it was so late.'

The scampering crowd ran past the old Grandfather with never a glance. They were looking for the Cuckoo, but he was so small, they never noticed his little coloured wings beating on a larkspur by the window.

Grandfather patted a fair little boy on the head, but he only shook his hair as if a wind had ruffled it, and ran after the others.

After them ran the Grandfather and the Cuckoo, but soon they left the children behind, hunting in the hedges, paddling in the streams, and away they went, through the village.

Leaning against a wall stood the policeman, and Grandfather stared at his fine helmet and bright buttons. But before he could speak the Cuckoo struck twelve again. Of course the Grandfather had to strike too, and his chimes rang through the village.

'Twelve o'clock!' exclaimed the policeman. 'I must get along to my dinner. Suet dumplings to-day,' and he hurried off home.

'I'm thirsty with all this striking,' cried the Cuckoo. 'Shall we go down to the river to drink?'

'Yes,' replied the Grandfather. 'I want to see the old river again. I used to lie by its side when I was a boy, and dream, and dream.'

They walked through the uncut meadow grass, thick with dog-daisies and blue crane's bill, to the great river. Grandfather's tight trousers were yellow with pollen, and the Cuckoo's wings were dipped in gold dust where he had fluttered among the flowers.

Then Grandfather sat down by the water's edge and cooled his toes, and the Cuckoo flew over the surface, pretending to catch flies like the swallows.

The water-rats came swimming up to talk to them, and a family of white ducks paddled down a side stream from the farm to ask the news. Brown rabbits ran from their burrows and hopped on Grandfather's knees, and little water wagtails flirted their tails as they walked sedately up to pass the time of day.

A pair of dippers left their young ones to look at the odd couple on the bank, and a gay kingfisher darted across the river to Grandfather's feet.

'How is Time on the river, nowadays?' asked the Grandfather.

'It's much faster than when you lived here,' said the water-rat. 'We have to move so quickly, and work so hard, it is night soon after it is morning.'

'But it's more exciting,' said the ducks. 'You should see us cross the road and hold up the traffic!'

'Tell us of long ago time,' said the rabbits, and they crowded round him, as he sat among the purple loose-strife and creamy meadow-sweet by the river brink.

So he talked and talked, and the day slipped by. Presently a cool wind blew, and the sun dipped down towards the horizon. The ducks' feathers were ruffled, and the water-rat turned up his collar.

'It's getting late,' said the Cuckoo, and he struck twelve. Grandfather chimed with his deep rich voice twelve times, too.

'Twelve o'clock?' cried the rabbits. 'What a joke! But the weasels will get us if we don't go home,' and they scurried off to their burrows.

The dippers flew off to their lonely, wailing babies, and the kingfisher and wagtails hastened to their nests. Only the water-rats remained.

'The sun hasn't gone yet, I can see it winking at us. Your time must be wrong, Grandfather,' they said.

'Yes, we've been wrong all day,' answered the old Grandfather, as he reluctantly drew his toes out of the water.

'But it's been a holiday,' said the little Cuckoo. 'We left Time behind.'

Grandfather stooped to the meadow grass and picked a great dandelion clock, round and pearl-coloured. He blew and blew, and the water-rats and the Cuckoo watched him.

'Eight o'clock,' said he. 'It's time the children were in bed.'

So he said good-bye to the river, and waved to the water-rats, who sat on the bank watching him. With the Cuckoo on his shoulder, he ran through the bending grass, along the lanes, by the village, to the house which anxiously waited their return.

They climbed into their empty cases, and closed

the doors. As soon as they were safely inside they both struck.

'One, Two, Three, Four, Five, Six, Seven, Eight.'

'Hello! The clocks are going again. They've stopped all day, and I couldn't make them go,' cried a voice.

'Time for bed, children.'

And, as the children went upstairs, the clocks sighed, and settled down to their quiet life again.

The Girl whom
the Wind Loved

It was cold and dark and frightening. The winter sun
had set hours ago, but the stars were hidden. They
didn't want to come out on such a gloomy night, so
they drew the clouds about them and shut their eyes.
So it seemed to the girl who walked home with her
head bent and her arms aching with the load of fire-
wood she carried. She lived with her grandmother in
the wood, and each day she left early to work at a
farm. She had to milk and churn, scour the buckets
and scrub the floors, and do all the work they gave
her. At night she came home, tired to the bone, but
eager to see her grandmother.

When she reached the cottage she thrust open the
door and dropped her load by the porch. The room
was nearly in darkness. The fire had only a glimmer
which shone on the old woman lying in her bed under
the window.

'Oh, Grandmother! How are you to-night? I am
so glad to get back. I've such a fine load of wood. It
will last us nearly a week. I'll get the fire going
quickly and the tea made. How are you, Grandmother?'

She kissed her grandmother and stroked the thin, withered cheek. Then she put some sticks in the hearth and blew up the fire with the great blow-bellows. The flame caught the wood and flickered over her pale, sensitive face, lighting up the auburn hair, and the snow-white skin. It sent its rays over the old woman's face and showed the deep burning eyes to the girl, whose heart was filled with pity and love and fear.

She filled the kettle at the water-trough by the door, and set it, hanging from the crook, over the fire. Then she swept up the hearth with swift, deft strokes and laid the table with a clean cloth and shining cups. All the time she chattered to the old woman, telling her about the day's work: the way she had scrubbed the dairy floor till the bricks shone red, and the way the cat purred at her and the dog licked her hand. Oh, she liked her work at the farm, hard as it was, and she liked the farmer's son, and she had brought home something the farmer's wife had given her.

She opened a packet and took out a pat of butter and some strong-smelling rich cheese, which she had helped to make. Her heart was heavy as she talked so cheerfully, for she could see that her grandmother was very ill.

'What shall I do without you?' she cried, suddenly kneeling by the sick woman. 'What shall I do?'

'Be a good girl and God will take care of you,' whispered the old woman, stroking her hair with frail hands. But a week later the grandmother died and the girl was all alone in the world. There was nobody to

welcome her home at night. The cottage was lonely,
but the girl wouldn't desert it. She loved every corner
of the little whitewashed house. She had been born in
the room under the thatched roof, she had played on
the stone floor of the cosy kitchen, which was so large
and empty with no grandmother there. Her own
father and mother had gone to a far land, and she was
to have followed them, but they had been drowned
and no one was left.

One night she sat alone in the cottage, sewing her
clothes. The fire flickered and crackled as the wood
burned merrily, and the lamp sent a warm glow over
the room. She was thinking of the farmer's son,
Robin, and the way he had helped her to carry a
heavy load.

Outside there was a roaring wind and the trees
shook their branches together with a rattle like bones
clicking, but inside it was warm and sweet with the
scent of lavender drying, and the girl pulled her chair
closer to the fire and put on another log. Suddenly
there was a bang at the door and a flurry of leaves and
branches.

'Who's there?' she called, opening the door a crack
and peering out. Nobody was to be seen. Only the
wind came rushing into the room, blowing and puffing at the fire. Then out it went and there was quiet.

The next night the same thing happened – a thud
and a bustle of drifting leaves.

'Who's there?' she called, opening the door a little
and looking round. Nobody was to be seen, but she
heard a sighing murmur, a soft whispering in the

trees. The wind came into the room, blowing, puffing at the girl's hair, touching her round cheeks with its cold breath. Then out it went and all was quiet.

The third night, when the muffled thuds came at the door, she took her candle, for the lamp was not lighted, and she waited and looked about her, demanding an answer.

'Who's there?' she called, holding the candle high. There was a huff and a puff, and the flame was blown out. It was a silent night, with no wind, but something rushed past her into the cottage. She looked round, but could see nothing except a whirling motion of leaves and paper.

'It must be the wind,' said she, and she stood there, half afraid, for no wind had been in the woods.

Then a voice came out of the darkness, a thin, high, reedy voice, clear as an angel's, sweet as honey, luring her as a fairy voice might do.

'Windflower! Windflower! Come away with me. Come out, beautiful one! I am the wind!'

So she put on her cloak, locked the door, and slipped the key in her pocket, for 'I do love the wind' she thought.

The wind blew her cloak tightly around her, and it wrapped her warmly in its folds. It put a strong arm to support her, so that, although it was now blowing with great force, she moved like a leaf caught in the embrace.

Her feet scarcely touched the ground as the wind blew her along, swinging her safely away from the trees and walls and obstacles. Her cheeks glowed in the wind's breath, her hair was caught up and it flew like a cloud around her head. Her eyes were shining like stars with the excitement of the rapid motion, and she leaned back against the powerful arms that upheld her and smiled up at the sky with its planets and moon. She was no longer a girl but a part of Nature, aware of feelings and movements outside her life.

'Where will you go, Windflower? What is your desire? What will you see?' asked the wind, with its round mouth close to her ear, and its cool kiss upon her cheek.

She laughed softly, enchanted by the magic of the moving air, and she whispered, 'Wherever you take me, Wind.'

'Are you happy?' asked the wind.

'Indeed I am,' she replied, as she was swung up in the air. So the wind took her over the countryside where she lived, running across the fields, keeping her feet from wet lands and marshes, as if a cushion of air were beneath her. It was like dream-flying, with no fear, only perfect confidence, and as they flew the wind told her stories of the journey, for it knew everything that had ever happened.

They passed a deserted house, and it blew with its strong breath through the empty windows and sighed down the broken chimneys, so that there was an eerie noise of pipes playing. Then it sang the story of the old house, and as it chanted the tale time was not and other days returned. Lights appeared at the windows, music sounded, and there was dancing and laughter.

It was the wedding of the eldest daughter, a hundred years before or more.

A coach stood in the drive by the door, and the heavily-caped coachman drank a mug of hot ale before the journey. The door opened, the bride came out with her husband, and away they drove into the night.

Then all faded away, the wind swept her on through the valley to an ancient manor, shattered by weather and by time.

Again time rolled back and she saw a queen there. Mary Queen of Scots stood at the windows of the hall. Her ivory face was wet with tears, and she held a little dog close to her heart.

The wind shook the window and spoke to her, and the Queen held up her arms to the boundless air.

'Take me with you, O Wind. Help me to escape,' she cried.

'Courage, courage,' whispered the wind, caressing her cheek with its pointed finger.

'Avenge me, O Wind,' sighed the Queen.

'Your vengeance will come,' said the wind, and then it flew onward, holding the girl firmly in its arms.

'Why didn't you help her?' asked the girl.

'She already has enough strength; she will conquer without my help,' said the wind. 'She will always have the world's memory. She is already immortal, the Queen of Scots.'

All night they travelled – sometimes across the water, when the girl stretched out her foot and touched the crest of a wave; sometimes across great towns, when the wind lifted her high above the roofs and swept her to the green earth beyond.

'Their ways are not my ways,' said the wind. 'My pathways are in the vast tracts of space, but I know all the doings down below.'

'Tell me,' said Windflower.

Then again the wind spoke, and sang stories of the people and their delights and sorrows, their joys and griefs, strange tales of long ago, and tales of that same night.

Windflower listened, scarcely understanding, her mind filled with the bliss of the dreamlike motion in the wind's arms, her heart ravished by the tales she heard in that clear angel voice which, knowing neither good nor evil, spoke in her ear.

The stars had faded from the sky when the wind at last took her back to the cottage. It loosed its grasp, and her cloak fluttered and unfurled from her body. She turned to thank it, but the wind was already mounting up.

'Windflower! Windflower!' it sang as it flew high, and she was left alone.

She felt in her pocket for the key and unlocked the door. The cat roused itself and came rubbing against her with hair on end. She slipped off her clothes and climbed into bed. In a moment she was fast asleep.

She was late at her work that day, and her mistress scolded her. Her head seemed full of nonsense, and she scarcely heard what anyone said, nor did she care.

She was thinking of the past night's adventure and her strange journeyings. Even if she told anyone they would not believe her. They would say it was a dream; but it was no dream, for she had brought back leaves and flowers she had snatched from trees as she passed: a scented magnolia from a garden, honeysuckle from a hedge, juniper from the hills. Flowers had been in a crown on her head, placed there by somebody in whose arms she had flown.

But the farmer's son, Robin, came to her and took the heavy bucket from her hand and walked by her side.

'You're different to-day, Mary,' said he. 'You have a look in your eyes which I've not seen before. What is the matter, Mary? Has anything happened to you?'

'Why, nothing,' she stammered. 'At least – Oh! Nothing you would understand.'

They walked on in silence, and then she said, 'Do you know a flower called the windflower, Robin?'

'Oh yes! It grows in our woods, a lovely thing, snow-white. It swings in the wind, I've watched it. It comes out in March and April. Why do you ask?'

'The wood anemone,' said she.

'You remind me of the windflower, Mary, if I may be a poet for once,' said Robin, half-laughing. 'You look like one who's seen the wind.'

'Seen the wind?' she cried, startled. 'Who could see the wind? It's invisible.'

'They say some animals can see the wind, dogs and horses can. They have the power. They see swirling columns of air, moving, it is said.'

'I wonder. I wonder,' whispered Mary.

'Don't you know the old country saying?' asked Robin. 'Who sees the wind sees past and future, like seeing what happened before you were born. Who sees the wind doesn't belong to this world.'

'You might see his footprints in the air, and feel his breath on your cheek and his arms round you,' persisted Mary in a low, trembling voice.

'His? His? Whatever's the matter, Mary? You are talking daft. Come with me and I'll show you the calf born last night. A cow calf, born when that high wind rushed over and the little cowshed seemed to shake with its force. What a wind that was! There were gusts big enough to blow off the roof.'

They went together to the calf place and leaned over to watch the baby calf, which slobbered and bumped its fawn-like head against them and tried to lick their fingers. Then the hand of the young man stole to that of the girl and held hers, and he whispered, 'Mary. Mary.'

She shook her head and ran off, back to the house, to her work in the dairy and kitchen.

The next night the wind came again, tap-tapping at the door, calling, 'Open, Windflower', and she threw wide the door.

'Put on your cloak. Come out! Come away, my Windflower!' chanted the thin, piping voice, and the girl obeyed.

The wind carried her off, wrapped in her cloak, and its strong arms held her from all the dangers and perils of land and air. As they flew over the hills and woods of England, it sang sweet songs to her, and the music was like an orchestra up in the clouds. Sometimes she thought it was the harps of angels in the heavens above, and sometimes that it was the pipes of Pan and all the ancient gods who once ruled the earth.

The exquisite airs lulled her to sleep, and the wind carried her home and laid her on her bed by the dying fire. When she awoke in the morning, on her head was a wreath of strange blossoms from another country, blue and silver and violet petals, with the scent of a far land.

She hurried to the farm and to her work, dazed and bewildered.

The farmer's son helped her with the rough tasks and watched her with eager, intent eyes, noticing the flush on her pale cheeks and the absent look which came to her as she stood at the wall gazing across the wide valley to the hills. She was dreaming of the voice of the wind, listening for the magical music, and she scarcely heard Robin's words when he spoke to her. She was thinking of the wind's caress and she never noticed the touch of the young man's fingers on her wrists. He sighed and turned away, and she stood motionless; but when a cloud shadow swept down the hills she started, and when the trees shook with a breath of wind she held up her arms, as if waiting for someone.

Each night the wind came and carried her on enchanting journeys. It wooed her with the songs of seraphs which it conjured out of the sky, and it decked her with the scented snowy flowers which were transparent under the moon's sickle. It kissed her with cold lips, and it opened magic casements to show her the wonders of fairyland. Yet she was never sure whether she loved it in return.

Each day the farmer's son courted her, and walked by her side through the fields. He spoke of country things, of foxes and fairs and flowers. He wooed her with his warm round whistle which called the birds, and he showed her the busy, intimate life of the small creatures of the earth, down under the ferns, hidden in hedgerows, cupped in petals, rose and tawny gold.

But she always walked as if in a dream, unheeding his words, her blue eyes on far-off things.

'She's bewitched, surely,' grumbled the boy's mother. 'Let her be. She's not for you at all. She's fey, for certain. She's maybe met a fairy man, or one of the ancient race come back to earth. She's not for you.'

The young man loved her dearly, and he determined to find out the cause of the enchantment of his sweetheart. He went to her cottage one night and waited in the garden. As he stood there a mighty wind rose out of nowhere and blew with such force he was brushed against the hedge and obliged to remain there. Surely the cottage roof would be blown off. Then he saw the door open and he heard a voice in the air cry, 'Windflower! Come to me, Windflower!'

'That's what she said – "Windflower",' murmured Robin.

The girl came out wrapped in her cloak, and

Robin tried to step forward, fighting against the power of the wind. He tried to cry out, but his words were blown back in his throat.

Mary was smiling at someone invisible to him, he could see her in the moonlight. She leaned back as if an arm were around her, she lifted up her face, and she was swept out through the gate and away over the fields, her feet not touching the earth, as if she were carried by an unseen spirit.

'Then it's true. She is bewitched,' groaned Robin, and sorrowfully he awaited her return. At daybreak there was a rush of air, a wild wind, and the trees bowed to the ground, the stream was blown into waves. He saw the girl drop to the earth, gently falling. Her eyes were shut, she wore a wreath of scented flowers, and in her arms were branches of marvellous orchids. She entered the house, without opening her eyes, and lay down. The wind died away and all was quiet.

Then Robin knew that his rival was the wind, the great invisible mighty wind, which rushes to and fro over the earth, and lashes the sea till the waves smash even the largest ships, the wind that is so powerful it can break the strongest tree as if it were a matchstick, the wind that is so gentle it can shake the rose and not displace a petal.

'I can do none of these things,' said he to himself. 'I can only love her. But my love is stronger than the wind's, for I love her more than life itself.'

So later on, when the sun was bright, and the farm was filled with the new life of spring, he left his ploughing and asked Mary to come with him to the hilltop.

They stood in the young bracken, looking over the valleys, and distant hills, and they waited, each secretly watching for the wind.

Robin whistled for it to come, as men have called the wind for two thousand years, and down it came rushing and roaring with a mighty bellow.

Robin stood firm and spoke to the element. He put his arm round the girl's waist so that the wind could not lift her without carrying him also.

'I love this girl and want to marry her,' he shouted to the wind, but the wind only shook its great head and bellowed and filled the air with strange wailing sounds like the cries of lost spirits.

'I love this girl,' cried Robin again, and he tightened his hold and Mary's fingers clung to his as the wind tugged at her body and tried to take her from him.

'Choose, Windflower,' sang the wind, and its voice had lost its beauty and become loud and wild as it beat against them and tore their clothes and lashed their faces, so that they clung all the tighter to each other. Mary hardly knew the wind in this guise. All its gentleness and fragrance had gone; it was hard and primitive and cruel.

'Which of us will you marry?' screamed the wind. 'An earth-man who will live with you in a cottage and give you pain and sorrow, old age and death, or the wind who will carry you to the mountain-tops and make you an immortal? You shall never die if you

marry me. You will see all the world – the hot
deserts of Africa, the Jungles of India, the ice-fields of
the Arctic, the fields of fairy – and you will have ever-
lasting bliss. Which will you have, my love or his?'

The wind tore at the bushes and stripped off their
leaves. The bracken was laid flat as if it had been
rolled, and the two had to kneel together, lest they
should be thrown down the slope of the hill. Robin
put his arms more tightly round the frightened girl
and spoke softly.

'I can only give you my love, and work and homely
things. I can give you children to bring up and cattle
to tend, and a house to keep, and a simple garden to
sit in. I can give you laughter and tears, and we shall
be poor, but also we shall be rich. Which of us will
you choose, Mary, my love?'

'Windflower! Windflower! Choose me,' called the
wind, but Mary kept her head bent.

'I will choose the earth and you, Robin,' she said
under her breath, half hidden as she knelt there, but
the wind heard her words. It stayed very still, it
listened, it died away. Only a breath of air seemed to
spiral upward, to spin away into the heavens.

So the two lovers went back to the farm, and soon
after they were married.

It was no life of luxury and peace, but a hard life of
toil, with plenty of laughter and only a few tears.
Children came to share their happiness and to bring
fresh burdens and delights. Sometimes, when the
wind was blowing, Mary told the children to listen
to its voice.

It flew over the farmhouse, calling 'Windflower!
Windflower!' Then it tapped at the door or rattled
the latch.

'Hark to the wind,' they laughed, snug by the fire.
'Hark. It wants to carry off our mother, but she won't
ever go. We are holding her tight.'

High up in the air the wind sang its songs, luring
them and enchanting them, and then it went, for it
had no more power over earth-love.

About the Author

Alison Uttley was born in December 1884 in
Derbyshire, and was brought up on a farm
some distance from a village, which meant
she dwelt in a real solitude of fields and woods.
She was never lonely – she had calves, lambs,
foals, dogs and her small brother for
companions, as well as country people, the
hedger, the ditcher, Irish haymakers and the
oatcake man.

She won a scholarship to a small grammar
school, and although her chief interest was
music, she turned to mathematics and
science and went to Manchester University,
gaining a degree in Physics Honours. After
going to Cambridge for a year, where she
studied English with pleasure and surprise, she
taught science at a London school, then
married a civil engineer and had a son.

The child listened eagerly to her stories, which
she had secretly been writing in an attic, and
she finally sent one to a publisher – who made
a book of it and asked for more, to her
astonishment. Since then her animal characters
Little Grey Rabbit, Hare, Squirrel, Sam Pig,
Brock the Badger, Tim Rabbit, Brown
Mouse, Little Red Fox have been compared
with the creations of Beatrix Potter.

Her first book, *The Country Child*, first
published in 1931, is still available in
Puffins.

Mrs Uttley died in May 1976.

Other Young Puffins by Alison Uttley

MAGIC IN MY POCKET
LITTLE RED FOX
MORE LITTLE RED FOX STORIES
THE ADVENTURES OF SAM PIG
SAM PIG GOES TO THE SEASIDE
SAM PIG GOES TO MARKET
SAM PIG AND SALLY
YOURS EVER, SAM PIG
ADVENTURES OF TIM RABBIT
THE LITTLE KNIFE WHO DID
ALL THE WORK

and in Puffins, for slightly older readers

A TRAVELLER IN TIME
THE COUNTRY CHILD

Who is he?

His name is Smudge, and he's the mascot o
the Junior Puffin Club.

What is that?

It's a Club for children between 4 and 8 who
are beginning to discover and enjoy books for
themselves.

How does it work?

On joining, members are sent a Club badge
and Membership Card, a sheet of stickers, and
their first copy of the magazine, *The Egg*,
which is sent to them four times a year. As
well as stories, pictures, puzzles and things
to make, there are competitions to enter and,
of course, news about new Puffins.

For details of cost and an application form,
send a stamped addressed envelope to:

The Junior Puffin Club
Penguin Books Limited
Bath Road
Harmondsworth
Middlesex UB7 ODA